FIELD & STREAM'S
Guide to the Outdoors

FIELD & STREAM'S GUIDE TO FISHING

T. EDWARD NICKENS
AND THE EDITORS OF FIELD & STREAM

Gareth Stevens
PUBLISHING

FIELD & STREAM'S
Guide to the Outdoors

FIELD & STREAM'S GUIDE TO FISHING

T. EDWARD NICKENS
AND THE EDITORS OF *FIELD & STREAM*

Gareth Stevens
PUBLISHING

CONTENTS

"If people concentrated on the really important things in life, there'd be no shortage of fishing poles."

—Doug Larson

Never Enough

Used to be, all I needed was a half day off work during the full moon of May. Drag my canoe 100 yards through the woods to the Carpenter Pond and whack bedding bluegills until it got so dark even the wood thrushes quit singing. No fish finder. No scent-impregnated plastics. Just a box of sinking black ants and popping bugs and a 4-weight fly rod that I made myself. Have I ever been happier with a rod in my hand? Probably not.

Back then, panfishing encapsulated all that was pure and simple and right in the world. These weren't fish whose shapes were embroidered on $85 shirts. These weren't fish you worshipped. These were fish you could catch with a worm or a cricket or a 49¢ lure. Fish you threaded onto a stringer and released into a frying pan. Not that I would give back a single day of chasing fish to the ends of the continent. I don't regret a moment of Arctic char fishing, for starters. Standing in the spray of a waterfall pouring over a lip of Yukon tundra, fighting a fish that had very likely never seen a lure or a man—that's an experience to keep in pristine mental condition.

The same goes for the memories of pig walleye transferred within minutes from the base of an Ontario waterfall to a black fry pan popping with hot oil. Or trout from Maine, Montana, Alaska, Arkansas. I'm a lucky man.

But I still can't turn my back on the blissfulness of a bluegill whopping a popping bug the color of hard candy. Most fishermen have experienced similar moments, I think. For most of us there's a place that we never forget: a certain crook in the river, a cove along the pond edge, a deepwater drop-off that always produced big fish. Or big memories. When it comes to fishing, one's about as good as the other.

Of all the outdoor pursuits, fishing may be the most knowledge-intensive. Every day is different. Every hour can change everything. Every species—every single fish—requires a specific set of actions and decisions designed to put forth what seems to be the simplest of requests: "Eat this, please."

There is so much to know. Twitch retrieve or slow strip? Let the bass run with the worm, or strike with every bump? Mayfly emerger or spinner or nymph or dun? Maybe not a mayfly at all? Rapala knot? Six-turn San Diego Jam? Rotten chicken liver or fresh?

For a lot of people, it's a little overwhelming. Those non-anglers can't get their minds around the unimpeachable necessity of five rigged rods for a single fisherman. Or a tackle box the size of an antique chest of drawers. (And we still wish we'd sprung for the next size up.) Do you really need the side-scanning sonar? A micro-scale pattern on the side of a minnow lure no bigger than a peanut? Can't you just go wet a line, for the love of Izaak Walton, without all the yammering about benthic invertebrates?

Let's be clear: There's not a thing in this world wrong with a cane pole and a bucket of red wigglers. But many of us suck up anything that smacks of a new cast or a new lure or a new way to rig a live shiner like carp rooting in the mud. We nurse a fetish for new knots. We will argue over the pros and cons of circle hooks until the bar closes and we are swept out with the dirt. We lie in bed at night with dark thoughts that would shock our mothers: *Maybe there's a better way to drop a weedless plastic frog into a black hole of lily pads, coontail, and who-knows-what. Maybe I should hold off on setting the hook for a count of three because fish in the salad get a mouthful of lettuce along with the lure. And maybe I'm not sticking the fish hard enough or holding the rod tip high enough to skitter the fish clear of the weeds. Maybe I can do better.*

That kind of knowledge doesn't exactly rank up there with that found in the Dead Sea Scrolls, but we want all of it we can get.

We're hooked.

So a lot has changed about fishing since my long afternoons on the Carpenter Pond. But here's what hasn't: You need fresh line on the reel. You'd better know how to tie a good knot. Keep your bait in cool water. Keep your shadow off the stream.

And you'd better get going. More than likely, someone else knows all about your honey-hole, and they just knocked off a half day of work.

—*T. Edward Nickens*

Ranger

1 FLIP A LURE THE FLORIDA WAY

When most people flip for bass, they let the line go, it hits the water, and if a fish hits the lure on the way down and then releases it, the angler never feels the bite. It's especially problematic in heavy grass—unless you know how to tighten your line before the drop. Cast right into the middle of a weed mat and let the lure drive a hole into the hollow beneath. But the real key is this: As soon as the lure hits the water, apply slight thumb pressure to the spool to control the drop of the lure. But don't just let it free-fall to the bottom. Set it on the mat and then lower it with your thumb. That will give you the ability to feel even the slightest of takes on the drop. —T.E.N.

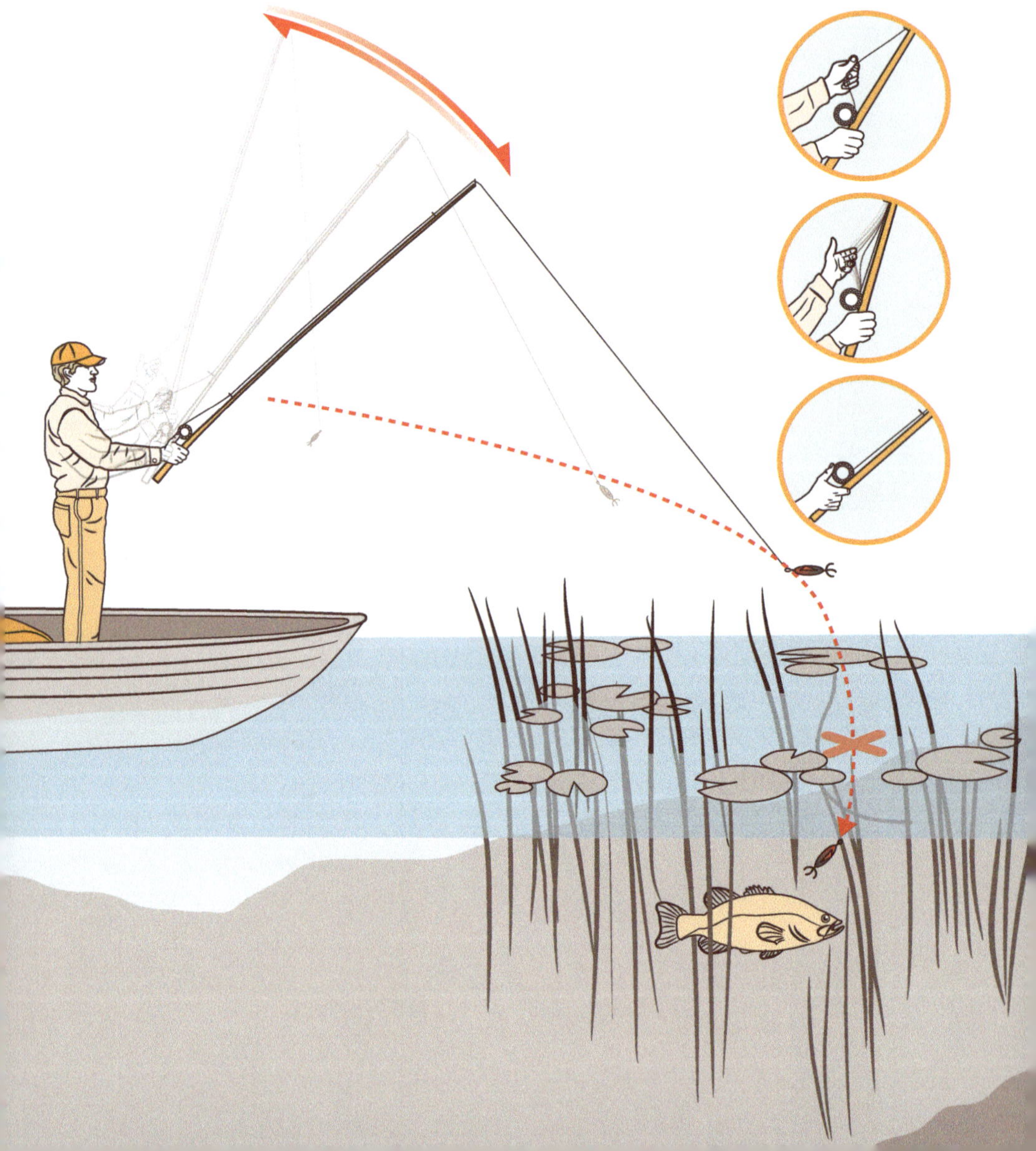

2 FISH WITH A SHINER

Florida is famous for wild live shiner fishing. "The fish chase those shiners to the surface," says fishing guide Todd Kersey, "and, oh, man, the world blows up right in front of you." Not in Florida? There are thrills wherever bass lurk.

GEAR UP Use a 4/0 live-bait hook, a standard egg bobber, and large baits—shiners between 6 and 10 inches. It's a handful, especially since the trick is to keep the shiner right above the grass. Sometimes you need 1/8 or 3/8 ounce of lead to keep the shiners down, but if you use lead, make sure you've got a real kicker for bait. The minnow needs to spook and run—bass love moving targets.

WORK IT The trick is in working the bite. A bass can eat a big shiner only headfirst—if it goes down tail first, the shiner's fins will get hung up in his throat. What happens is this: The bass blows out of the water, grabs that shiner, and starts buzzing drag off the reel. Your first instinct—to lock down and let him have it—is the worst thing to do. Let the fish run, and when he stops to turn that shiner around in his mouth, that's when you hit him. Sometimes it's 5 yards. Sometimes it's 35. You never know. —T.E.N.

FIELD & STREAM CRAZY-GOOD GRUB

3 TRY A POACHED FISH

A good meal is essential on a good fishing trip. You can poach your fish and the recipe is simple.

STEP 1 Build a good fire.

STEP 2 Lay out a sheet of heavy-duty aluminum foil that is two and a half times longer and deeper than your biggest fish. Drizzle the bottom of the foil with olive oil and then add a 1/2-inch-thick layer of sliced green onions. Add a cleaned fish to the top of the pile and souse it with a few ounces of chicken stock. Roll up the foil, sealing the fish, onions, oil, and stock in a tight pouch.

STEP 3 Place the pouch near hot coals for about 15 minutes for a decent eating-size walleye. The onions will char. The stock will steam. The fish will flake with a fork. You will eat like a king. —T.E.N.

4 FLY CAST TO FICKLE POND TROUT

When conditions are perfect, one of trout fishing's signature endeavors is fly casting to brook trout rising to surface flies in remote backcountry ponds. But when the stars haven't lined up over his favorite brookie water, Maine guide Kevin Tracewski has learned how to fool the pond squaretails. Here's how.

Anchor the boat fore and aft as far away from any structure, such as a suspended weedbed, as you can cast. Using a heavy sinking line, make a long cast. Strip out 10 feet of line and shake it through the tip-top guide. Drop your rod tip to the water—and then do nothing. The line will sink to form an underwater L, dropping straight from your rod tip and then extending out toward the structure. "Count down, say, 10 seconds before starting a retrieve," Tracewski says. "The belly of the line will pull the fly through the sweet spot until it is nearly to the boat." If you don't get a hit, cast again and count down 15 seconds before retrieving, then 20 and 25. —T.E.N.

5 TRACK GRASSLINES WITH SONAR

Big Bass + Underwater Grass = Reel Bearings Shrieking in Pain. How to complete the equation in unfamiliar water? Follow what Texas guide John Tanner does:

STEP 1 "I look for coots hanging out in a cove or along the shoreline," Tanner says. "Ninety-nine percent of the time, they're over vegetation." Point the bow of your boat toward the birds and idle in. Keep a sharp eye on the console sonar. As the outer edge of the grassline begins to show on the bottom contour, cut the motor and turn the boat parallel to the grassline.

STEP 2 "Now I jump up front, drop the trolling motor down, and pick apart the grassline edge with the front sonar," Tanner says. You want to follow the very margin of the vegetation, so watch the bottom contour. If the sonar shows grass starting to get tall, steer away from it. If the grass gets sparse or disappears from the sonar, turn into it. Start fishing on the outside edge of the vegetation before working your way in. —T.E.N.

6 LAND A BIG FISH BY KAYAK

The stakes are higher when you're fishing from a kayak. The craft's instability makes it tougher to manage how much pressure you put on the fish, not to mention the fact that landing a serious pike or muskie means you have to be wary of teeth in addition to hooks. Here's how to handle the heavyweights.

PREPARATION The key is letting the fish get tired enough to handle—but not so worn out as to prevent a healthy release. Straddling the kayak (1) will give you leverage and better balance. Make sure that all landing tools are within reach but out of the way (2). Because you're so low to the water, a net is rarely necessary. With the fish beside the boat, turn on the reel's clicker. Keep at least a rod's length of line out (3) since too much line tension loads up the rod and could result in you getting yourself impaled by a hook.

EXECUTION It's usually when you go to lift a pike or muskie that they are going to thrash about. Keep your eye on the lure at all times. Holding the rod in one hand, grab the back of the fish's head, just behind the gill plates (4). Pin especially big fish against the kayak. Once the fish is stabilized, pop the reel out of gear and set the rod in a rod holder (5). Use a fish gripper to lip the fish (6). Slide your hand below the belly to support the fish as you lift it out of the water. —T.T.

7 MIMIC THE TASTIEST CRUSTACEAN

Big trout can't resist the stop-and-drop flight path of a fleeing crayfish. Colorado guide Landon Mayer perfected this retrieve while targeting largemouth bass, and it's a coldwater killer as well. Use a weighted crayfish pattern for best results.

STEP 1 With the rod tip pointed at the surface of the water—or submerged as deep as 6 inches in the water—feel for tension on the fly. Then strip in 1 to 3 feet of line in a single, abrupt motion that lifts the fly off the stream bottom and into the water column, like a crayfish trying to escape a predator.

STEP 2 Pause long enough to feel tension from a strike or until you no longer feel the fly as it settles back on the bottom. The drop often puts up a little puff of sand, just like a crayfish hitting the dirt.

STEP 3 Repeat the abrupt strip. When a fish hits, set the hook with a pinch-lift strike: Pinch the fly line against the cork handle with your index finger and lift the rod hand sharply to a 45-degree angle. —T.E.N.

8 PIMP A RIDE FOR YOUR FLY

Dark, gnarly undercut banks often hold the biggest trout in the stream. But getting a fly under those banks, and getting it deep enough to prompt a strike from a monster trout, requires expert fly casting and a precise presentation. Or a leaf. Here's how to use fall foliage to float your fly into the perfect position.

STEP 1 Hook a weighted streamer or nymph fly, such as a Woolly Bugger, to the outermost edge of a dry and buoyant tree leaf.

STEP 2 Carefully sneak upstream to a position above the undercut bank you're looking to target. Then strip off a few feet of line and ease the unconventional rig into the current.

STEP 3 Pay out line as the leaf drifts to the target area. As it approaches to within 2 to 3 feet of the hole, give the line a sharp snap back with your line hand to rip the fly from the leaf. Your weighted streamer will drop into the current, which will carry the fly under the bank and down to your target trout. —T.E.N.

9 CHUM BREAM WITH A DEAD RACCOON

Old-timers did whatever they had to do to fill a stringer. Used to be, they'd nail a hunk of a dead cow to a tree over a farm pond, and sit back while the sun shone down and a thousand flies showed up at the party. These days using a roadkill raccoon is more common, but chumming with maggots still works. The process is pretty much the same as in days gone by—find an expired mammal of medium size, hang it over a pond, and come back in a few days. Bream that have swarmed to feed on the falling fly larvae will smack anything you cast. Just don't tell your dinner guests about your fishing partners. —T.E.N.

10 READ TROUT LIKE AN UNDERWATER BOOK

Find glare-free viewing lanes of shade or darker colors reflecting on the water surface, such as shadows from streamside vegetation. These are windows of opportunity for sight-casting to trout. Got your viewing lane? Good. Here's what to look for.

WHITE "O" Analyze every speck of white on the stream bottom. An on-off glint of white is the inside of a trout's mouth. A broken pattern of white glints is a feeding trout (a).

MOVEMENT Look for a fish that moves slightly, then returns to the same location in the stream. That's a feeding fish (b).

SILHOUETTE Imagine a sketch of a fish with a heavy outline filled with color. Now remove the outline. That's the target: a ghostly underwater smear (c). —T.E.N.

11 DETECT LIGHT BITES

Even experienced anglers struggle with the light takes of walleye. It's especially tough with jigging. Nine times out of 10, a jig bite feels as if you're nudging weeds or about to get hung up on something. The rod just loads up a bit and feels a little heavy. That's likely to be a walleye, but people will end up pulling bait away from fish half the day. You're better off setting the hook. If it's a fish, you're a genius. If not, what did you lose?

To catch the bite, hold the rod at a 45-degree angle away from you, not straight out in front. Hop that jig as you bring the rod from the 45- to a 90-degree angle and then reel back to the original 45-degree angle again. This step is critical. Why? Because if you hold the rod straight out, you won't be able to see the line hesitate or the rod tip bump. —T.E.N.

FIELD & STREAM-APPROVED KNOT #1

12 TIE A CLEAT HITCH

Quick and easy, the cleat hitch is one every angler should learn, whether you own a boat or not. Take a full turn around the cleat and then make two figure-eight loops around the cleat horns. Finish with a locking hitch: Twist the line so the free end passes under itself. Snug it tight and loop or coil remaining line out of the way. —T.E.N.

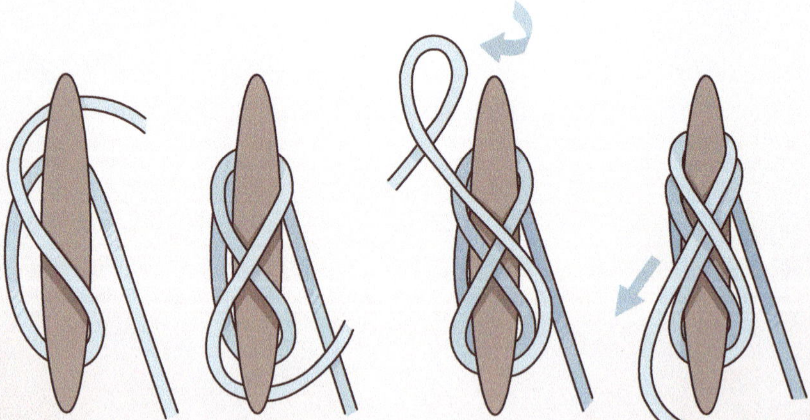

13 FOOL THE WARIEST TROUT IN THE RIVER

Large brown trout don't behave like small ones. Here's what sets them apart: —K.D.

SMALL BROWN	VS	TROPHY BROWN
Juvenile brown trout eat frequently and typically focus on invertebrates like worms, aquatic nymphs, and smaller insects.	*Forage*	Large brown trout eat fewer, larger meals. They key on calorie-rich foods like baitfish, mice, leeches, and nightcrawlers.
Smaller brown trout are in tune with natural bait and fly presentations.	*Attraction*	Motion on a fly or lure often piques the interest of a large brown.
Smaller browns feed at various times, including midday.	*Feeding Times*	Large browns feed in low light, often in the dead of night.
Small browns cling to "ideal" trout habitat where insects are plentiful and easy to feed on. You will occasionally find these fish sharing the riffles with rainbow trout.	*Location*	Trophy browns travel to hunt for food, but they will defend the heart of the run. Large browns can survive and thrive in sections of the river with warmer water and fewer insects.
Small fish will forgive any casting faux pas. If you see a fish strike at your lure or fly and miss, and then come back, assume it's small. They are also sensitive to overhead shadows and motions but are forgiving of underwater vibrations.	*Spookiness*	You won't fool a monster brown trout if you make a bad cast. And if you rip that bad cast out of the run, that stretch is finished for the evening. Large browns will shut down entirely if they sense any of your movements.
Smaller brown trout are influenced by river currents as the battle ensues.	*Fighting Ability*	A hooked big brown isn't very affected by current and will head for cover.

14 HARVEST NATURE'S BAIT SHOP

If you have a shovel and a lawn, you've got all the worms you need. But that's not the only productive bait around. The creek you fish can supply its own—for free. (Just be sure to check bait-collection regulations in your area before heading out.) —J.C.

IN-SEINELY CHEAP

You probably have most of what you need to make your own seine at home. First, get a 6x9-foot piece of nylon mesh from a fabric shop. Find two old broom handles and position one at each end of the net. Staple the mesh to the handles, leaving a few inches of net hanging past the tips at the bottom. Finally, attach some ½-ounce fishing sinkers a foot apart across this bottom edge with zip ties. You're ready to drag.

Good bait shops carry some of these critters, but expect to pay a lot more for a dozen hellgrammites than you will for 12 shiners, or a pound of crayfish.

1 HELLGRAMMITES
Rare is the fish that won't devour one of these nasty aquatic larvae. Pick them off the bottom of submerged rocks by hand or stretch a seine across a fast-water section of the creek and flip rocks upstream. The current will then flush the bugs right into the net.

2 MINNOWS
Minnows are easier to catch off the main current. Approach from midstream with a seine and corral the school against the bank as the net closes. If the bait is thick and the water is fairly shallow, a quick swipe with a long-handled dip net will also work.

3 CRAYFISH
Choose a stretch of slow to moderate current; flip rocks and scoop the crayfish with a dip net. You can also stretch a seine across the creek and walk toward it from upstream while splashing and kicking rocks to spook crayfish down into the mesh.

4 SALAMANDERS
Often overlooked, this bait is like candy to bass and big trout. Look for them under larger rocks near the water's edge. The most productive rocks are dry on top but cool and moist underneath. Moss-covered rocks farther up the bank are prime spots, too.

5 GRUBS
Find rotten wood near a creek bed. Peel away the bark to expose the soft, dead wood, or poke around in the dirt underneath, and you'll probably find some fat white grubs. Find a trout or crappie that won't eat them and you've done the impossible.

6 GRASSHOPPERS
The best way to catch all the hoppers you'll need is to walk through the tall grass that likely will be flanking almost any given stream. Use a butterfly net to skim across the tips of the blades and you'll have a dozen or more hoppers in a flash.

15 FISH A BREAM BED

For sheer action, few angling pursuits can touch spring-spawning bluegills. In ponds and lakes, look for sandy flats near deep water—they'll be Swiss-cheesed with beds. In rivers and streams, check out woody cover near hard bottoms and shallow water—a single dinner-plate-size crater can hint at dozens more nearby. And no matter where you live, look for excuses to skip work on the full moons of spring and early summer, when bluegill spawning peaks and every cast can land a fish.

PRE-SPAWN 'Gills are suspended off shore of their spawning flats, so key in on creek channels near hard sloping ground and mid-lake humps. Back off into 5 to 15 feet of water and use small slip bobbers to suspend wax worms, wet spider patterns, and red wigglers in the water column. Retrieve a half-foot of line and then hold while the bait settles.

Fly anglers can trawl for pre-spawn bluegill with a weighted fly trailing a black ant.

SPAWN As water temperatures nudge 65 degrees F, the females move to the bream beds, followed by the bucks. Spawning will peak when the water hits about 75 degrees F. You can't go wrong with crickets, worms, crankbaits, sponge spiders, hairy nymphs, and tiny spinners. The key is stealth. Stay as far from the beds as you can and still comfortably cast.

Cast to the outer edges of the spawning beds first and then work your way in.

POST-SPAWN Breeders need recovery time, and move into deeper water adjacent to the beds. Target tangles of roots, treetops, lily pads, and deep channels where the bottom falls steeply. Try weighted bobbers to detect the lightest bites. And don't give up when the bites go flat. Many bluegill spawn multiple times, so check bream beds as the next full moon nears.

One-pound trophy 'gills are not worried about bass predation, so you'll want to hunt for them on the outside edges of shady structure. —T.E.N.

gold-ribbed hare's ear

red wiggler

cricket

popping bug

black ant

mini-tube spinner

16 PATCH A KAYAK WITH DUCT TAPE

Launching kayaks off riprap landings and concrete boat ramps can be really hard on a boat. When this treatment leads to a cracked hull, here's how to fix that kayak and get back to chasing stripers in 30 minutes.

STEP 1 Stop the crack from enlarging by drilling a hole at each end of the split. Rub the cracked area with sandpaper, and clean it with a damp cloth. Let dry.

STEP 2 Heat the patch area with a hair dryer until it's nearly hot to the touch. Neatly place duct tape over the crack, overlapping it by 2 inches. Push out air bubbles. Now heat the patch with the hair dryer until small wrinkles form under the tape. Use a spoon to press as hard as you can, starting in the middle and working to the edges of the duct tape. Don't drag the spoon. Pick it up, press down, and roll toward the tape edge.

STEP 3 Repeat with three other layers, overlapping them by about 1/4 inch.

—T.E.N.

FIELD & STREAM CRAZY-GOOD GRUB

17 FRY FISH STREAM-SIDE

You fish. You fry. This is the sacrament of the river trip, and here is how you get from a cooler full of fish to a riverbank communion.

At home, fill a break-resistant 1-quart plastic water bottle with peanut oil. Pour 2 cups of breading mix into a 1-gallon, zip-seal bag. Stuff it, along with a second empty bag, coffee filters, paper towels, and a baggie of Cajun spice mix, into a second plastic water bottle. Your fry kit is complete. At the campsite, it'll be quick and easy to put it all together. —T.E.N.

STEP 1 Pour enough peanut oil into a skillet to cover the fillets' sides but not spill over their tops. Place the pan on two long parallel logs and build a fire in between. You don't need coals. For precise flame control, keep smaller branches handy.

STEP 2 Season the fillets liberally with Cajun spice and toss them into the empty plastic bag. Shake well. Add bread crumbs and, using your fingers, work the breading into the cracks. Shake off the excess. Now get ready—here comes the magic.

STEP 3 The oil should be almost smoking hot. Ease in a small piece of test fish. You want a rolling, sputtering boil around the edges. Nothing less will do. Gently add the other pieces but don't crowd the pan.

STEP 4 Give the fillets 2 to 5 minutes per side. When the fish turns the color of caramel, turn carefully—and only once. It's done when you can flake the fillet all the way through. Drain fillets on paper towels. Let the excess oil cool and then strain it back into its bottle using a coffee filter to reuse.

18 GET THE CATCH OF THE DAY

Throughout the trip we'd had moments of total fish chaos—multiple hookups, the Cane Pole hole, outrageous rainbow trout. But fishing remote Alaska isn't about the numbers, or the variety of species. It's about the way the fish are seasoned with fear, sweat, miscues, and the mishaps that make for an authentic trip in authentic wild country.

On the night before our scheduled pickup, we camped at the juncture of the Aniak river and a long, sweeping channel. After setting up the tents, Colby Lysne cooled his heels. His toes were swollen, chinook-red, and oozing pus from day after day of walking in waders. "I can't even think about wading right now," he stammered. "I'm just gonna lie here and fish in my mind."

The rest of us—Scott Wood, Edwin Aguilar, and I—divvied up the water. The others headed off to hunt rainbows down the side channel, while I hiked upstream to fish a wide pool on the main river. Since I'd lost my rods and reels when our boat flipped, I fished a cobbled-together outfit of an 8-weight rod with a 9-weight line. It was a little light, but heavy enough for the fish we'd landed over the last few days. In an hour of nothing, I made 50 casts to an endless stream of oblong shapes. Then suddenly my hot-pink fly disappeared. Immediately I knew: This was my biggest king, by far. The salmon leapt, drenching my waders, then ripped off line and tore across the current.

The rod bent deep into the cork, thrumming with the fish's power. I'd have a hard time landing this one solo, so I yelled for help, but everyone was gone.

So I stood there, alone and undergunned, and drank it all in. It no longer mattered if this was my first or fifteenth or thirtieth king salmon. What mattered was that wild Alaska flowed around my feet and pulled at the rod, and I could smell it in the sweet scent of pure water and spruce and in the putrid tang of the dying salmon. I felt it against my legs, an unyielding wildness. What I felt was part fear, part respect, and part gratitude that there yet remained places so wild that I wasn't so sure I ever wished to return.

Then the big king surfaced 5 feet away and glimpsed the source of his trouble. At once the far side of the river was where the salmon wanted to be, and for a long time there was little I could do but hang on.

—T. Edward Nickens, *Field & Stream*, "The Descent," June 2007

Alaska
STEARNS

19 CAST INTO A TORNADO

Heavy lures require a rod at least 7 feet long, with action in the tip to help load the forward section. Here's how to launch into a gale.

STEP 1 Holding the rod with both hands, bring it all the way behind you and stop when it is parallel to the water surface. Keep the rod horizontally behind you, knuckles up, and chill. Now, let 'er rip.

STEP 2 Right-handed casters should have their weight on the right foot. Shift your weight to the left as you begin to power the rod tip overhead. Instead of carving an arc in the air, shift your right shoulder forward to flatten out the top of the stroke. Accelerate through the cast, arms extended out. Then hold the pose, Madonna. It'll take a while before the lure lands. —T.E.N.

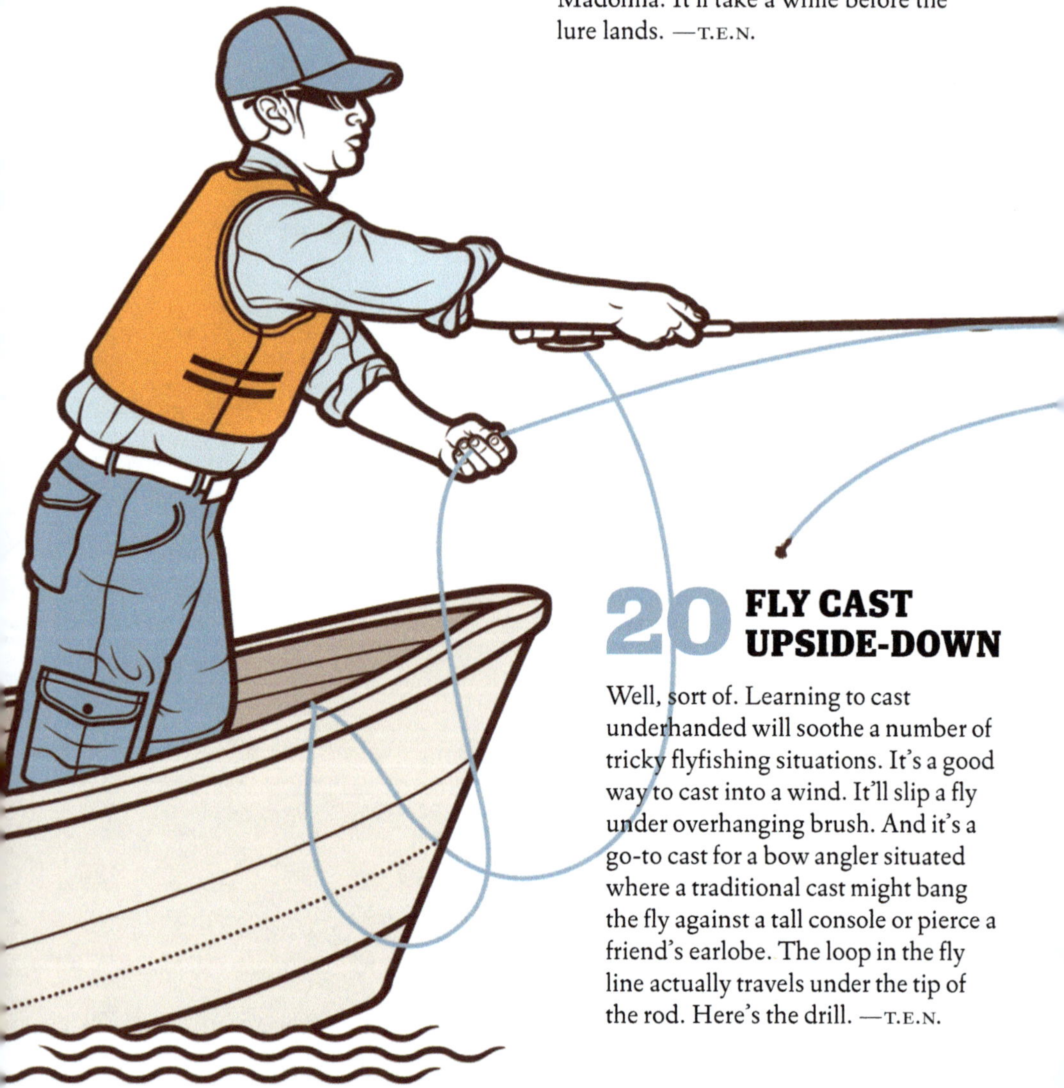

20 FLY CAST UPSIDE-DOWN

Well, sort of. Learning to cast underhanded will soothe a number of tricky flyfishing situations. It's a good way to cast into a wind. It'll slip a fly under overhanging brush. And it's a go-to cast for a bow angler situated where a traditional cast might bang the fly against a tall console or pierce a friend's earlobe. The loop in the fly line actually travels under the tip of the rod. Here's the drill. —T.E.N.

21 UNHOOK YOURSELF

Depending on how deeply you've sunk the barb into your own flesh, your choices are good, bad, and worse. If the barb protrudes from your epidermal layer, removing the hook is a snap. Just cut the hook shank below the barb and back the hook out. If the barb is embedded but is still close to the skin surface, it's time to grin and (literally) bare it: Push the hook point the rest of the way out, cut it off behind the barb, and then put it in reverse. A deeply embedded hook point requires a nifty bit of macramé, line lashing, Newtonian action-reaction physics, and a quick, courageous yank. It's not so bad. Really.

Here's how. First, double a 2-foot length of fishing line (at least 10-pound test) and slip the loop around the midpoint of the bend in the hook. Hold the line ends between the thumb and forefinger of one hand and wrap the line around the opposite wrist, leaving a few inches of slack. With the free hand, press the hook eye down against the skin to keep the barb from snagging. Don't let the hook shank twist. Grasp the line sharply, line it all up nice and straight, breathe deep, and yank. Really. —T.E.N.

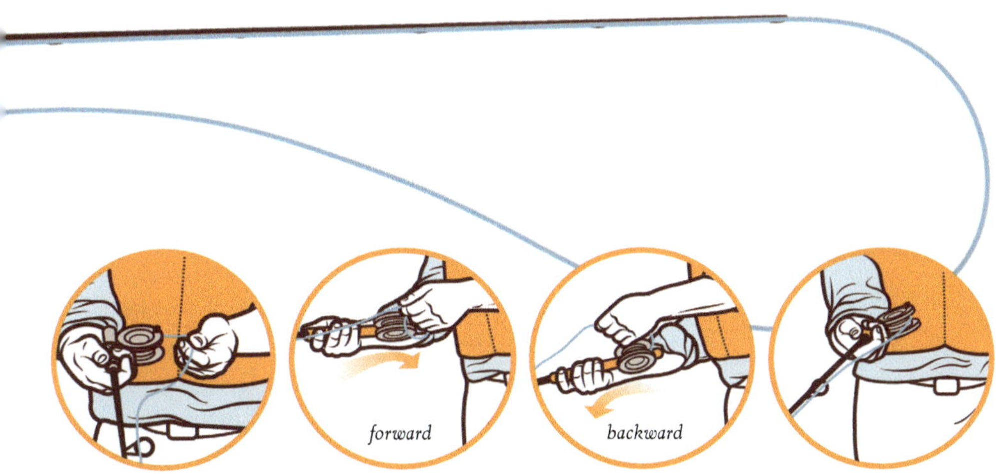

STEP 1 Start with a side cast, with the rod held nearly horizontal to the water's surface. Turn the rod grip almost 90 degrees so the butt rests against your forearm. This gives you leverage.

STEP 2 Begin your false casting. At the end of each forward and backward stroke, you need to lift the rod tip up slightly. This will form the essential upside-down loop.

STEP 3 Deliver the fly with a strong forward cast. This should be powered with a strong flick-and-stop of the forearm; the motion is as if you were throwing a Frisbee™.

22 TROLL WITH SURGICAL PRECISION

Often, maintaining a precise speed is the key to successful trolling, and often it's best to go very, very slowly—sometimes less than a mile per hour. You always want to troll with the wind, but the problem comes when a stiff breeze pushes the boat too fast. Here are three ways to slow it down.

LOCK When using a trolling motor, put the main engine in gear to lock the propeller. This can slow your forward speed by 0.1 or 0.2 mph—which can make a critical difference when fishing for sluggish walleyes.

TURN Turn a bow-mounted trolling motor around and slip it into gear. Now it's pushing backward, and you can use the big engine as a rudder.

TRAIL Clip a drift sock to the bow eye and let it trail under the boat. Most people only use drift socks while drifting, but this trick can save the day. —T.E.N.

23 THROW A CAST NET

Despite its reputation, throwing a cast net requires neither voodoo nor the gyrations of a matador. These simple steps are the stripped-down basics, good for nets up to 6 feet wide, which should cover most freshwater needs.

STEP 1 Cinch the rope around your right wrist and coil all the rope in the palm of your right hand. Hold the top of the net with your right hand, with a few inches of gathered net sticking out from the bottom of your fist. Hold your right hand at waist height.

STEP 2 With your left hand, reach down and grab a lead weight; it should be the one that's hanging closest to directly below your right thumb. Bring it up to your right hand and grasp it between your thumb and index finger. Pick up another weight that's an arm's length from the first. Hold this between your left thumb and index finger.

STEP 3 Next, point your feet toward the water; rotate your upper body to the right; and in one smooth motion, swing your right arm out at a slightly upward angle. Release your right hand first and then your left. The net should open into a circular shape and drop. —T.E.N.

24 MISS A RAFT-EATING BOULDER

When you're dealing with long cumbersome oars and a craft that has all the maneuverability of a 14-foot-long wet pillow, oaring a raft doesn't come naturally. Here's how to manhandle these river monsters.

SETUP Sit just aft of center so the oars are centered in the middle of the raft for maximum pivot power. Adjust the length of the oars by starting with 4 inches of space between the handles.

COILED SPRING A proper oar stroke is part leg press, part upper-body row. Stay compact and don't overextend your body or arms. Reach too far with the oars and you lose control.

A GOOD DEFENSE A back-ferry stroke is the rafter's best move. [1] To skirt a rock or obstacle, use oars to swing the bow at a 45-degree angle to the obstacle and back-row. [2] Now fine-tune raft placement by pushing with one oar (a) and pulling on the other (b) to realign the boat, then slip by the rock in the current.
—T.E.N.

25 SCALE FISH WITH BOTTLE CAPS

Do you drink soda from a bottle? Can you scrounge up a piece of wood about 6 inches long? Do you have two screws and a screwdriver? If so, you can assemble this handy-dandy fish scaler. —T.E.N.

26 SKIN A CAT IN A JIFFY

Don't pout when a catfish pounces on your jig. Cleaning Mr. Whiskers is not as difficult as some people think.

STEP 1 Hold the catfish belly down and make two shallow slits through the skin: one should nearly girdle the fish's head from pectoral fin to pectoral fin, and the other should run from the top of this cut past the dorsal fin and down to the tail.

STEP 2 Grasp a corner of the skin flap firmly with pliers, and pull down and across the body all the way to the tail. Repeat on the other side.

STEP 3 Remove the head by bending it first toward the tail and then the stomach and then pulling it free of the body.

STEP 4 Remove the entrails by opening up the body cavity with a knife.

STEP 5 Fry and eat with a smile. —T.E.N.

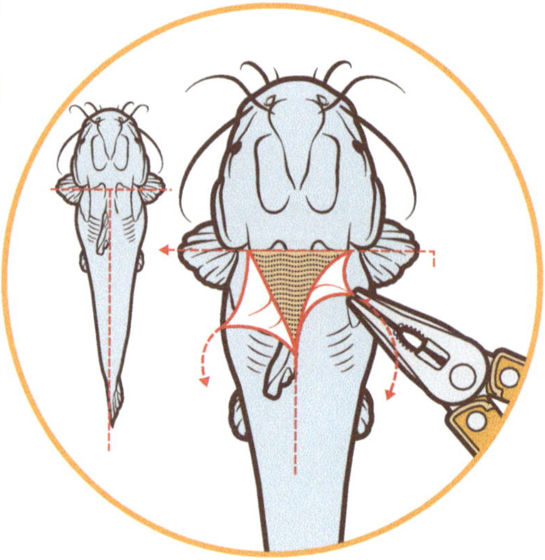

27 CAST WITHOUT DRAG

There's a step-by-step process to master the short, accurate slack-line cast. First, choose the target, be it a rising fish or a rock. Too many people skip this part, and the game is over. Account for current speed and drag and guesstimate the exact spot where you want the fly to land. Second, as you cast, carry 2 to 3 feet of extra slack in your line hand. When you carry through that final forward stroke, aim precisely at your target spot. As the fly reaches the target, release the slack line, and, when the line straightens out, check the rod tip abruptly. That will cause the line to recoil and drop in a series of S-curves that will defeat drag. —T.E.N.

28 STORE BULK FISHING LINE

Most manufacturers will tell you that storing line for up to a year is no problem, but there are some significant caveats. First, long-term storage should always take place on bulk spools, not on spools of a quarter pound or less. The larger diameter of bulk spools will cut down on the problem of line memory, in which the coiled line retains loops that will snarl your casts come spring. You should also be careful about storing lines in a garage. Garages are often full of chemical vapors that can degrade monofilament and fluorocarbon lines, so you don't want your spools anywhere near cleaning agents, solvents, automobile fluids—just the kinds of thing you typically keep in the garage.

Equally important to line stability is a stable environment without large temperature fluctuations, so unless your garage is heated, it's better suited for beer than for bass string. A simple solution: Stack bulk spools in a couple of shoeboxes and jam them up on the highest shelf in the hall closet. —T.E.N.

30 DRAG FISH OUT OF A CAVE

They are deep and dark as Grendel's lair, which is why Grendel-size trout, snook, and redfish like to hole up in undercut banks. Follow these tips to foil a cave dweller.

Cast a plastic tube bait, lizard, or other light lure with an embedded hook point onto the bank a few feet upstream of the undercut. Jiggle it into the water and let the current carry it under the bank. Leave a bit of slack so the lure sinks, reel in quickly, and jerk the rod tip to impart action. Stop to let the lure slow down a bit, enticing a strike. —T.E.N.

29 STICK A SHORT-STRIKING SALMON

Short-striking fish can drive a fly angler batty, a situation well-known to landlocked salmon fishermen who must contend with conflicting currents in larger rivers. What to do when you don't have a fly with a trailing hook handy? This: Let the accidental back cast level out behind you and then forward cast to the same spot where the fish spat out your lure. Keep the line fairly taut but let the fly drift and sink naturally, as if it were mortally wounded by the original chomp. Give it 5 seconds and then give it a good twitch. That's often enough to entice a salmon to show up for a second helping. —T.E.N.

31 SKATE A FLY WITH A RIFFLE HITCH

A riffle hitch can be a very effective tactic. It is a knot that enables a fly to skim and skitter across the water surface, leaving a V-shaped wake that often results in a strike. That's called "skating a fly," or, as it is otherwise known, "Holy moley! Why haven't I tried this before?"

STEP 1 Attach tippet to the fly with an improved clinch knot.

STEP 2 Next, you're going to want to add a half-hitch behind the eye of the hook, taking care to pull the tag end of the leader straight down. Add a second half-hitch in front of the first one. Pull the tag end of the leader straight down and snip. The half-hitches can be placed as far down the fly as the gape of the hook for a variety of actions on the water.

STEP 3 Cast down and across. The fly floats higher in the water column and will skate across the surface film. Spincasters can use this technique with the addition of a casting bubble. —T.E.N.

FIELD & STREAM-APPROVED KNOT #2

32 TIE A RAPALA KNOT

The Rapala knot is a winner because the wraps, which are ahead of the initial overhand knot, relieve stress where the standing line enters the rest of the knot. Also, line passes through the overhand knot three times, which serves to cushion the standing line.

STEP 1 Tie an overhand knot six inches above the tag end of your line. Thread the tag end through the lure eyelet and then through the overhand knot.

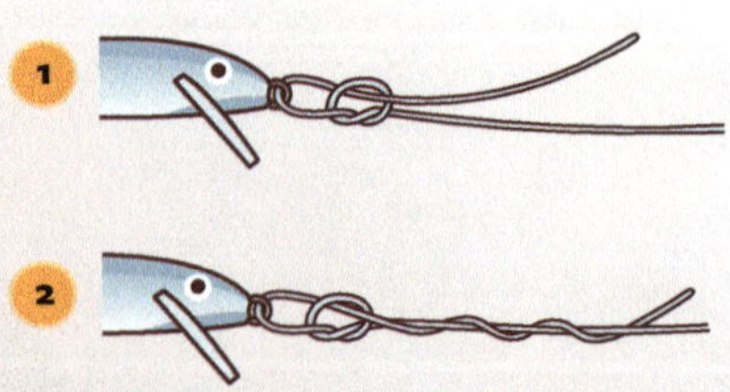

STEP 2 Next, take the tag end and wrap it three times around the standing line.

STEP 3 Pass the tag end through the back of the overhand knot.

STEP 4 Run the tag end through the new loop you formed in Step 3.

STEP 5 Lubricate and tighten by pulling on the tag end, main line, and lure. —J.M.

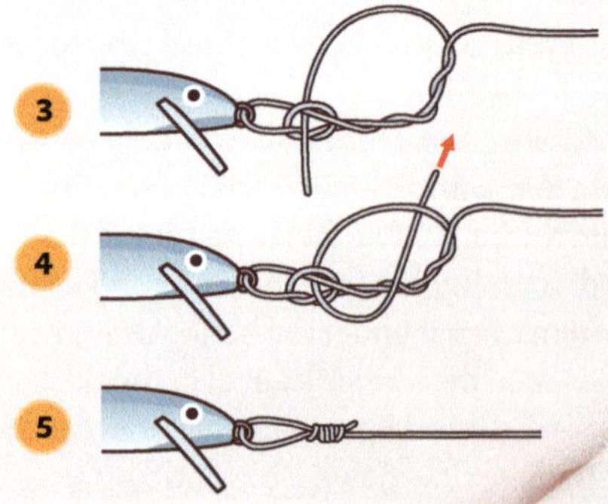

33 CROSS AN EDDY LINE FOR STACKED-UP FISH

It's a fact that strong eddy lines below rapids and boulders hold fish, but it's also true that it takes a good eddy turn to place a boat in casting position. Remember the word PAT: *power, angle,* and *tilt*.

POWER The canoe has to be moving forward in relation to the current speed. You need enough momentum to cross the eddy line.

ANGLE Position the canoe at a 45-degree angle to the eddy line. Aim high in the eddy—higher than you want to go because the current will carry you downstream. Maintain angle and speed until the center of the boat crosses the line; then the bow paddler should draw to turn the boat into the eddy.

TILT Two guys in a loaded boat sitting on the seats risk a quick flip as the eddy pushes on the hull. You have to lean and bank the boat into the turn; the stronger the eddy, the harder the lean. —T.E.N.

1
2

34 GET SALTY WITH YOUR BASS SKILLS

Your largemouth tactics can come in handy during a week at the beach. You can adapt them to fishing in a saltwater marsh—and you could be pulling trout, flounder, and redfish from the water instead of sulking at your 10th round of miniature golf.

GEAR UP Spool a medium-weight spinning reel with 8- to 10-pound monofilament line. Stay away from braided lines; the mouths of marsh fish such as trout and flounder are surprisingly soft, and you'll need some stretch to keep from tearing hooks out. For a basic tackle kit, carry a dozen leadhead jigs in white and red, and a handful of curly-tailed jig bodies in colors that imitate shrimp and in chartreuse (1).

POUND THE STRUCTURE Every dock piling, patch of oysters, bulkhead, rock pile, and abandoned crab pot is a potential reef full of fish. Target these areas just as you would fish around the tree stumps in the farm pond back home (2).

AMBUSH HOLDING FISH Analyze each stretch of tidal current as if it were a river and then fish accordingly. Marshy points, undercut banks, and deep water beside oyster beds and sandbars are great places to cast for fish holding in the lee of the tides (3).

BE THE BAIT In most cases, your lure will mimic shrimp or small baitfish. Lift and twitch your rod tip to allow the lure to rise and fall (4).

CHECK THE TIDES Tides affect fish movements and feeding times to a huge degree because moving tides sweep a buffet of prey—shrimp, small crabs, and baitfish—into the feeding lanes of holding fish. In most coastal regions, two high tides and two low tides come in and out of the marsh each day. Fish the hour or so before and after each change of tide. —T.E.N.

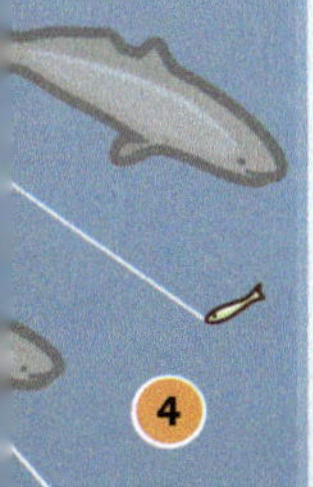

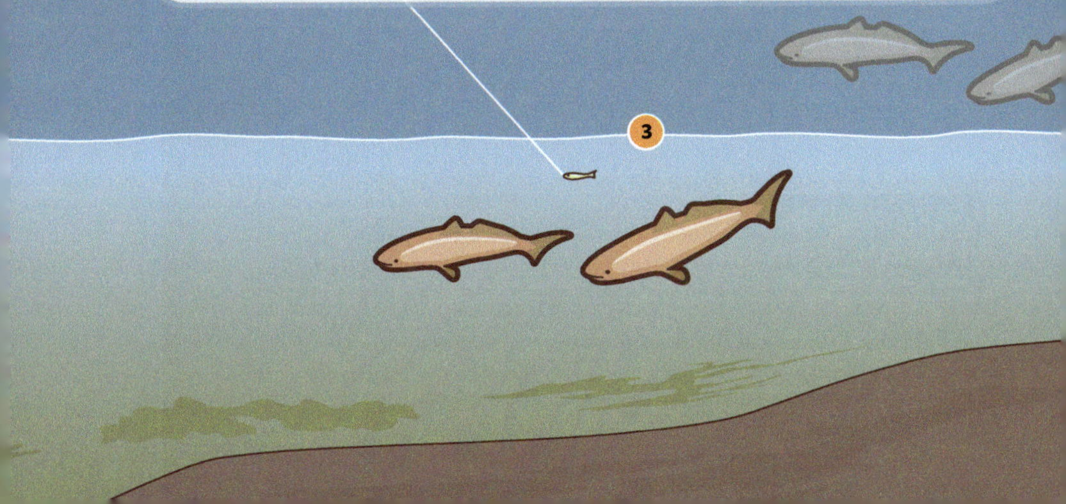

35 CHOOSE A REEL

At the most basic level, a fishing reel is simply a device used to store, deploy, and retrieve fishing line. But in the hands of a skilled angler, a strong, well-designed reel is a tool used at every step in the quest to catch a fish. It helps vary the speed and action of the lure, lets a light-biting fish take the bait without a hint of your presence, halts the strongest drag-screaming run, and controls the line when the fish is just about in hand. Here are the three most common reel types. To know them is to love to put them to hard use. —T.E.N.

BAIL Serves as a line pickup device to return the line evenly on the spool after the cast.

DRAG ADJUSTMENT KNOB The drag is a system of friction washers and discs. Front-mounted drags are typically stronger than rear-mounted drags.

SPOOL Holds the fishing line. A skirted spool covers the main reel shaft like a skirt to prevent line entanglement.

GEAR HOUSING Protects the internal gears that connect the handle to the spool.

SPINNING REEL

Spinning reels have fixed spools that do not rotate—the line uncoils from the front of the spool, pulled by the weight of the lure. Since the cast lure doesn't need to have enough force to spin a rotating spool, spinning reels can utilize very light lures—ultralight spinning reels can handle lures as feathery as $1/32$ of an ounce—and backlash is rarely an issue. The downside to spinning reels: stopping a cast isn't a straightforward task. And spinning reels are notorious for twisting line. It's best to pump the rod up and reel on the way down to minimize twist.

REEL FOOT Slides into mounting slots of the rod's reel seat.

ANTI-REVERSE LEVER Prevents the reel handle from turning as line is playing out.

HANDLE Activates the gears to retrieve line. Spinning reels come in a wide range of gear ratios, which is the number of spool revolutions to the number of gear handle revolutions. High-speed retrieve reels have gear ratios in the 4:1 class or higher. Lower gear ratios support more cranking power.

BAITCASTING REEL

The spool on a baitcasting reel revolves on an axle as it pays out line. By applying thumb pressure to the revolving spool, an angler can slow and stop a cast with pinpoint precision. Baitcasting reels require skill and practice and are a favorite of bass anglers, many of whom insist the reels afford more sensitive contact with the line than spinning reels. Baitcasters get the nod from trolling fishermen, too, for the revolving spool makes it easy to pay out and take up line behind a boat and also reduces line twist.

SPOOL TENSIONER Is a braking device to reduce spool overrun and resultant "bird's nest" line snarls.

LEVEL-WIND GUIDE Attached to a worm gear, this device moves the line back and forth across the face of the spool evenly to prevent line from getting trapped under itself.

FREESPOOL BUTTON Allows the spool to turn freely for the cast.

SPOOL Holds the fishing line.

STAR DRAG Adjusts tension on a stacked series of washers and brake linings that make up the reel's internal drag.

HANDLE The latest upgrades offer ergonomic grips with grooves for better control.

FLY REEL

Flyfishing reels don't revolve during a cast, since fly anglers strip line from the reel and let it pay out during the back-and-forth motion called "false casting." In the past, fly reels have served largely as line-storage devices with simple mechanical drags. Advancing technology and an increase in interest in flyfishing for big, strong-fighting fish have led to strong drag systems that can stop fish as large as tarpon. Other recent developments include warp- and corrosion-resistant materials and finishes and larger arbors—the spindles around which the line is wrapped—that reduce line coils and help maintain consistent drag pressure.

DRAG KNOB Adjusts drag tension. Some smaller reels have a spring-and-pawl drag, while reels for larger fish sport strong cork and composite disc braking systems.

FRAME Holds the spool. A weak frame will warp, causing friction as the spool revolves.

HANDLE Unlike spinning and baitcasting reels, rotating the handle of a fly reel typically turns the spool a single revolution.

ARBOR The spindle around which the fly line is wrapped. Many modern reels have larger arbors that help recover line more quickly when a fish swims toward the angler.

SPOOL Many reels are fitted with removable spools. Having different fly lines ready on a number of spools allows an angler to switch tactics more quickly.

36 CARRY A TACKLE BOX AROUND YOUR NECK

Trout anglers figured this out ages ago: Why weigh yourself down when all you want to do is blitz a local creek? Bass busters can do the same. Turbocharge a flyfishing lanyard with the items listed below, and you can work your way around a pond unencumbered.

Start with a neck lanyard with at least five disconnects. If your lanyard comes preloaded with floatant holder, small nippers, or other trout-specific tools, remove them. Then load it up with the following essentials.

PLIERS Look for the lightest fishing pliers you can find. Some models even float (1).

FILE A short hook file. Yes, you need one (2).

SPINNERS AND JIGS Stuff a small fly box with a few spinners and jigs and whatever else you might need once you're on the pond (3).

SCISSORS Super-braid scissors will cut heavy gel-spun and super-braid lines (4).

MULTITOOL Look for a small multitool that can do business as a mono clipper, a screwdriver, and a bird's-nest detangling aid (5). —T.E.N.

1

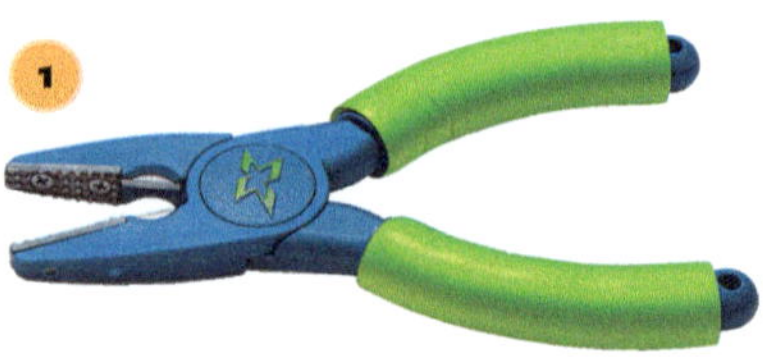

2

3

5

4

37 FINE-TUNE A WACKY WORM FOR PENNIES

Rigging a wacky worm the traditional way—driving the hook through the middle—results in a lot of expensive baits flying off the hook or hanging up in brush. Here's how to solve two sticky wacky-worm problems at once.

SHOP IT Take your favorite wacky-worm baits to a hardware store and start shopping: You need black rubber O-ring washers like you'd use on a leaky kitchen sink, and they need to fit snugly on the body of your worm. While you're there, pick up a few small black panel nails or brads.

RIG IT Snip off the nail head with wire cutters and insert the long part of the nail into the head of the worm. Slip the O-ring down to the midpoint of the worm. Thread your hook through this O-ring, so that the hook point is in line with the worm.

FISH IT Cast into the salad with confidence. The rubber O-ring absorbs the force of the cast, preserving the bait. And the weight will make the worm fall slightly headfirst, carrying the hook with the point facing up. You'll snag less often—and catch more fish. —T.E.N.

38 FISH UNFISHABLE WEEDS

Pulling hog bass from heavy slop requires the right gear. Long, stiff rods have the muscle to horse them out of weeds. Baitcasting reels have the winching authority. Braided superlines cut through heavy vegetation and have near-zero stretch, which means they make hooksetting much easier.

Drop a weedless plastic frog right into the mess. Wiggle, skitter, pause, and pause it some more. Watch for a bulge of water behind the frog, created by a stalking bass waiting for open water, but be ready for an out-of-nowhere explosion. When the fish hits, hold off on the hookset for a count of two or three. Then stick it hard and keep your rod tip high. Try to get the fish's head up and pull it out of the very hole it made when it surfaced. Keep up the pressure to skitter the fish across the slop and turn back all attempts it may make to head for the bottom. —T.E.N.

39 TUNE LURES

Test each crankbait or spinnerbait by making a short, 20-foot cast. Hold your rod tip straight up, and reel. A lure that runs more than 5 or 6 inches off to one side needs tuning. To tune a crankbait, replace bent split rings. Straighten out hook hangers with needle-nose pliers. If all appears fine, hold it so that the lip faces you and use light pressure to bend the line tie in the direction you want the lure to run. Retest. Repeat until you're satisfied. For a spinnerbait, hold it with the line tie pointing at you. Look straight down the top wire; it should be situated directly over the hook and aligned with the shank. If not, bend it into place. If the spinnerbait rolls left or right during the retrieve, bend the top wire in the opposite direction. —T.E.N.

FIELD & STREAM-APPROVED KNOT #3

40 TIE A BLOOD KNOT

Join the tippet to the leader with this classic flyfishing knot.

STEP 1 Cross the tag ends of the lines, and leave 6 to 8 inches overlapping. Hold where the lines cross, and wrap one tag end around the other standing line four to six times.

STEP 2 Repeat with the other line, and bring the tag ends through the gap between the wraps, making sure to go in opposite directions.

STEP 3 Pull the lines, moisten, and draw the knot tight. —T.E.N.

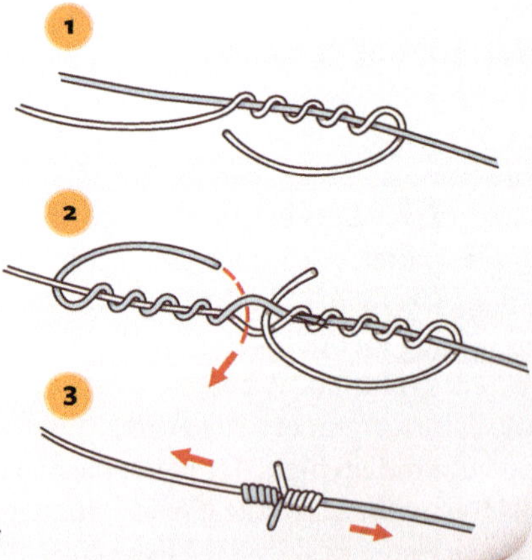

41 STICK IT TO SHORT-STRIKING FISH

Steelhead regularly short-strike, one of the many reasons they drive anglers crazy. Teach nimble-lipped steelies a lesson with a trailer-hook streamer pattern, tied with bunny strips, Flashabou, and other materials: a great fly for largemouth and striped bass, pike, and other fish with a big appetite. (Check local laws for multiple-hook regulations.)

STEP 1 Make a loop with approximately 5 inches of 20-pound Dacron backing. When the fly is completed, the tail materials should not extend past the trailer hook, so decide now how long the fly will be. Thread the loop through the eye of an octopus hook for drop-shot rigs, with an upturned eye.

STEP 2 Lay the two tag ends of the Dacron loop along opposite sides of the shank of the fly-pattern hook. Next, rotate the loop so the dropper hook point rides up. Apply drops of a superglue or epoxy to secure the loop to the hook shank. Wrap very tightly with thread.

STEP 3 Build up the body of the fly in whatever pattern you choose. —T.E.N.

42 AVOID SINKING YOUR BOAT IN HEAVY WATER

Some lakes dish up big, nasty rollers day after day, but just about any lake can throw up bruising water in the right—or wrong—wind.

You don't want to pound through endless 4-footers in an 18-foot boat, so tack across the rollers as long as they're not breaking. As the roller approaches, run down the trough parallel to the crest, as far as you can or need to, and slide over the crest into the trough behind it. Then turn the bow straight into the swell and ride up and down the rough spots until you need a break. It's slower going, but it's better than getting beat up for miles. —T.E.N.

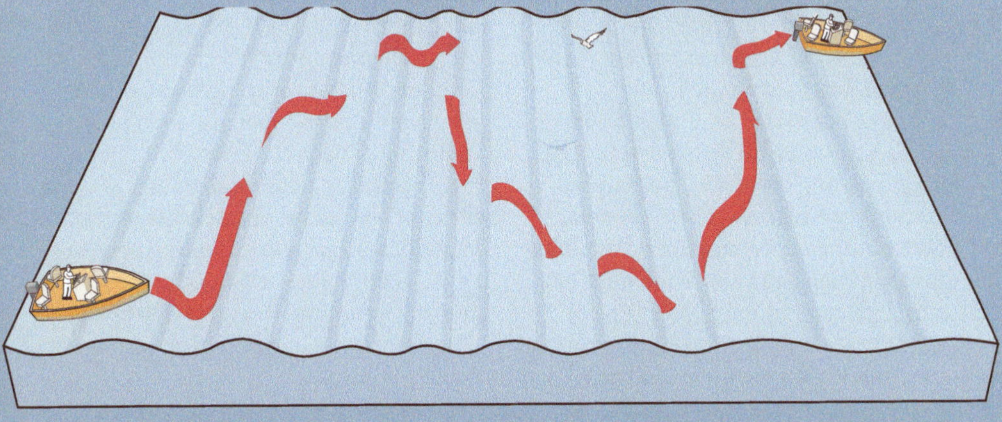

43 CATCH A CAT WITH PANTYHOSE

Dough balls are notoriously difficult to keep on a hook. Here's a way to solve this problem. Make dough balls by mixing bloody hamburger and flour, liver and dough, or hot water and cornmeal mixed with licorice and sugar. Toss one into the toe of a pantyhose leg and tie it off with a piece of dental floss snugged next to the dough ball. Now tie another piece of dental floss next to the first knot; snip the hose between the knots. Turn the remainder inside out. You'll have an encased hunk of catfish bait, and the pantyhose is ready for you to make some more. —T.E.N.

44 FLYFISH FROM A MOVING BOAT

This skill is not just about firing off the quick cast. Flyfishing from a moving boat is both a mental and a physical game. You have to see things coming and process the future, and you have to simultaneously perform very well and adapt to what's happening right now and right in front of you. It's not something that you can just jump into a boat and do well the first time, but the angler who can put together the right strategy will catch 25 percent more fish than the guy who can't.

The first step is to be acutely aware of what's happening on the river for the next 50 yards downstream. You need to be watching two places at once: your strike indicator or your fly, and the river coming up. Your mind and your vision must be constantly monitoring them both. Acquiring this ability is like learning to drive, but it's flip-flopped; with driving, you constantly watch the road but monitor the mirrors to have a sense of what's behind and beside you.

After all of that comes the hard part: devising a kind of choreography of upcoming casts to take advantage of the lies—the little foam lines, pockets of still water, current seams—that are in that next 50 yards. And the next and the next.

And you have to keep that diagrammed in your head while you work the water at the boat. The trick to casting from a drift boat is throwing a bit more slack into each cast to compensate for the fact that the line slack doesn't last very long when you're moving, the boat is moving, and the river is moving. To do this, carry a little extra line in your line hand, and, right at the end of the power stroke, you actually feed that loop of slack line into the cast. Shake it through the guides at the end of the stroke, and you'll gain an extra second or two of drag-free float—critical in drift boat fishing. —T.E.N.

45 STEER BIG TROUT AWAY FROM DOWNED TIMBER

CHECK THE RUN Apply pressure above the trout by lifting the rod from the butt section—not the tip. This will have the effect of forcing the fish into a head-shaking posture and blunts the surge.

STILL GOING? Don't lift the rod tip. Sweep the rod in the same direction the fish is moving—the momentum and line movement guides the fish away from the obstruction.

KICKING YOUR BUTT? Stick your rod tip into the water and free some slack line. You want the tip to carry the fly line and leader low enough to clear the sunken timber. The current will keep enough tension on the belly of the slack line. Once the fish clears the trees, bring the rod tip up and to the side to guide the fish out. —T.E.N.

FIELD & STREAM-APPROVED KNOT #4

46 TIE A SIX-TURN SAN DIEGO JAM

Because the San Diego jam uses wraps around both the tag end and standing line, the knot has a better cushion and is stronger than clinch knots, which wrap around only one strand. The improved clinch owes its popularity to its old age: It was one of the first knots that worked well with monofilament line, a WWII-era invention. Knots have since advanced—it's time to learn to tie the San Diego.

STEP 1 Thread the line through the hook eye and double it back 10 inches.

STEP 2 Wrap the tag end over itself and the standing line six times, moving toward the hook.

STEP 3 Pass the tag end through the first open loop at the hook eye.

STEP 4 Thread the tag end through the open loop at the top of the knot.

STEP 5 Lubricate and tighten by pulling the tag end and standing line, making sure the coils stay in a spiral and don't overlap. —J.M.

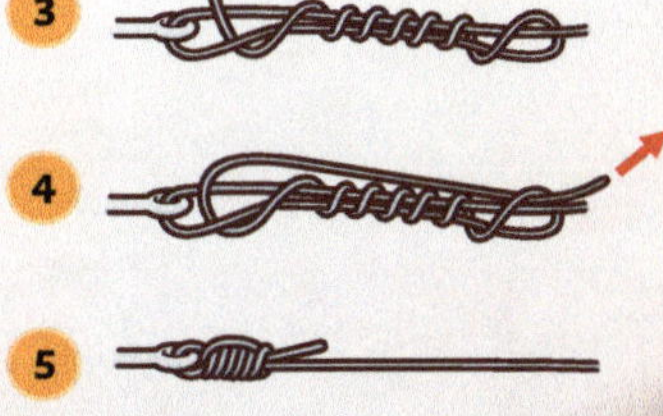

47 CATCH A MUSKIE AT BOAT SIDE BY DRAWING A FIGURE EIGHT

Wisconsin muskie guide and pro angler Jim Saric puts the finishing touch on muskies following a lure to the boat with an aggressive sweep of the rod tip in a figure eight. "Muskies, like pike, will follow a lure, but they're not nearly as aggressive," Saric says. The figure eight is a final enticement performed by the angler before lifting the lure out of the water for another cast. To visualize this, think of a roller coaster. As you move the lure side to side, it also moves up and down. That 3-D action can really turn on a fish.

"You don't want a lot of line out because you'll lose control of the lure," Saric says. "Also, be sure to maintain lure speed throughout the maneuver. If you slow down as you make a turn, the blade will stop turning and a fish will lose interest." Saric emphasizes that you should perform the figure eight on each cast. It needs to become routine so you do it properly every time.

"I've seen fish wiggle their tails and flare their gills near the boat, and you can't help but think, Here it comes!" he says. "And what happens is an angler may stop to look at the fish." This loss of lure action can cause the muskie to turn away.

Try to set the hook across the face of the fish so that it rests securely in the jaw. "The basic idea is to initiate the fight close to the boat to maintain more control over the fish." But, Saric notes, "Big muskies will do what they do."

GET HIS NUMBER Cast and retrieve as usual, until there's 18 inches of line between the lure and the rod tip (1). Dip the rod tip 6 inches into the water (2). Draw a complete figure eight (3). The directional change can incite a reluctant muskie to strike. Keep in mind that a big muskie can come from behind you. You won't see it until it strikes (4).

THE TACKLE Saric recommends 7- to 8-foot fast-action casting rods. The longer length lets you cover more water and reduces upper-body movements that can spook fish. Spool a baitcasting reel with 80- to 100-pound-test braided line. "You have the opportunity to hook a 50-pound fish," Saric says. "This is no time for light line." —S.L.W.

48 MASTER THE CANOE PADDLE

The much-lauded J-stroke kills a canoe's forward momentum. Try this: Finish off a traditional forward stroke by rolling both wrists over and away from the boat. This turns the paddle blade perpendicular to the water surface, like a rudder. Here's how:

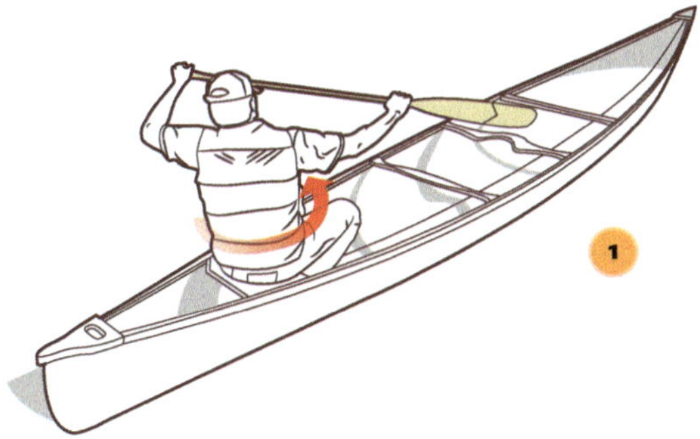

STEP 1 This is a must: Rotate the upper body away from your paddle side. Your shaft hand grips the paddle above the blade, and that arm is nearly straight. Your grip hand is pulled back toward your nose. Get it right, and you should be able to see under your grip-hand arm.

STEP 2 As the paddle catches the water, unwind the upper body and pull the paddle back. Use the entire upper body, not just your arms. This power stroke stops when the paddle blade reaches your hips. After that, you're just pushing water up and wasting energy.

STEP 3 A powerful forward stroke turns the canoe, so now it's time to correct course. As the paddle reaches your hips, the thumb on your grip hand should be pointing away from you. Now rotate your wrist so that your thumb points straight down. This turns the paddle blade perpendicular to the water surface, like a rudder. Now give a slight push away from the gunwale as you bring the blade out of the water for the next stroke, and the bow tracks back in line. You can correct course and make all but the sharpest turns without losing forward speed. —T.E.N.

49 TURN POOL NOODLES INTO CATFISH JUGS

Here's a way to recycle foam pool noodles into a simple new twist on this time-honored summer pastime. Just remember to keep a noodle or two intact—you'll need something to grab should you sink your boat with whiskerfish.

NOODLE NINJA Cut one 5-foot pool noodle into five 1-foot sections. (You'll be able to store five noodle-jugs upright in a 5-gallon bucket—enough to keep you plenty busy.) Wrap one end of each with three wraps of duct tape; this will protect against line cuts. Use a large darning needle or crochet hook to string a 4-foot length of stout mono (60- to 100-pound) or trotline cord through the tape wrap. Tie off one end to a washer or bead, pull it snug, and tie a three-way swivel to the other end.

RIGGED AND READY To the swivel's lower ring, attach a length of 20- to 40-pound mono that's long enough to reach the bottom. To the third ring, tie in a 4-foot dropper line of 20-pound fluorocarbon and a circle hook. Anchor the rig with sufficient weight for the current—any old chunk of iron or half a brick will do. To reduce line twist while wrapping line around the noodle for storage, use a barrel swivel near the weight.

CAT FOOD A small live bluegill, large wads of nightcrawler, or cut bait will catch just about any catfish.

GLOWING RESULTS If you fish at night, run a strip of reflective tape around the noodle on the opposite end from the line. It'll show up in a flashlight beam.

CATFISH RODEO For a complete blast, use a 4-ounce weight on the bottom and free-float all the noodles as you monitor the action from the boat. Nothing says summer like chasing down a bunch of catfish noodles gone wild. —T.E.N.

50 CONTROL YOUR WAKE

Many boaters believe that just slowing a boat down decreases its wake at a rate equal to the loss of speed. But there's more to it than that. Here's the right way.

STEP 1 Decelerate 50 yards ahead of the no-wake zone. Move all of the passengers to the bow to pull more of the stern out of the water.

STEP 2 Cut the power gradually and completely and then bump the throttle to maintain steering speed. The most common wake mistake is simply slowing down to a transition speed in which the bow is up and the stern is still plowing through the water.

STEP 3 You're going to want to go as slow as possible whenever you're in narrow channels. Waves rebounding off the shoreline are damaging to underwater structure. —T.E.N.

51 SHARPEN A CIRCLE HOOK

The same qualities that enable a circle hook to embed its point into a fish's mouth also prevent the angler from easily sharpening the cutting edge of the hook. Place the bend of the hook in a small bench vise. Make light strokes from the point of the tip toward the barb with a high-grade diamond file (a rotary tool will overheat the metal). But be careful not to oversharpen—the point of a circle hook is to let its geometry do the work.

—T.E.N.

FIELD & STREAM CRAZY-GOOD GRUB

52 MAKE FISH FRIED RICE

Fish fried rice is everything most other fish dishes aren't. It requires a single pan, one spoon, and less time than you need to land a 10-pound striper. Go low-tech with this recipe as is or dress it up with slivered carrots, oyster mushrooms, or a tablespoon or two of Thai fish sauce. And it's a snap for shore dinners: Mix the soy sauce, ginger, and spices in a small bottle at home and complete in the field.

INGREDIENTS

1/4 tsp. minced ginger
1/2 tbsp. Chinese five-spice powder
4 tbsp. soy sauce
2 tbsp. peanut or sesame oil, divided
1 1/2 pounds fresh fish fillets, cut into bite-size pieces
1 cup green peas (rehydrate if using dried peas)
1/4 cup sliced green onions
2 cups rice, cooked and chilled
2 tbsp. fresh parsley, chopped
3 eggs

Mix ginger and five-spice powder with soy sauce. Set aside. Heat 1 tablespoon of oil in a wok or large skillet, and stir-fry fish fillets 1 minute. Add peas and onions, stir-fry 2 minutes. Add soy sauce and spice mixture; stir well and remove from pan. Heat remaining tablespoon of oil and add rice and parsley. Stir-fry one minute. Scrape rice mixture to sides of skillet, leaving a doughnut-shaped hole in the middle. Add eggs, scramble, and cook for one minute. Add fish and vegetable mixture, mix thoroughly, and continue stir-frying until eggs are cooked, about 2 to 3 minutes. —T.E.N.

53 STICK A FISH WITH A FLY FROM A MILE AWAY

Flyfishermen moving from freshwater trout to quarry such as river stripers, migrating shad, and most saltwater fish need to learn how to strip-strike. Simply raising the rod tip on armor-mouthed or deep-running fish won't set your hook. Nor will it do the trick when you're dredging striper holes with weighted lines or battling currents and tidal rips with long lengths of fly line. Here's what to do once you feel a fish on the line.

STEP 1 Keep the rod tip pointed at your fly at all times.

STEP 2 Release the pressure on the line with the same rod-hand finger you use to control stripping.

STEP 3 Strip line in with a hard, quick, jabbing motion—anywhere from a foot to your full extended reach, depending on how much line there is in the water. If there's a lot of slack in your fly line—a deep belly from fishing weighted lines, or swooping curves caused by river or tidal rips—then you'll need to strip-strike while lifting the rod tip in several short pumping motions. Or follow up a strip-strike with a so-called body strike by holding the line taut and rotating your body to sweep the rod to one side. You can also pull the line and rod in opposite directions—a strip-strike offspring known as a scissors strike. —T.E.N.

54 STEER LIVE BAIT TOWARD A HIDDEN LUNKER

Savvy anglers fine-tune hook locations on live shiners to guide the bait into different kinds of structure. Hooked through the lips, a shiner has a tendency to swim back to the boat or stay in one place. A hook at the base of the dorsal fin creates bait action as the minnow tries to swim away, and it will splash on the surface. Hook the minnow near the anal fin—close to the spine—to make it dive. To get the bait under floating mats of vegetation, hook it just above the anal fin. The shiner will swim away from the boat, and by gently lifting and dropping the rod tip, you can get the bait to swim deeper. —T.E.N.

55 MAKE YOUR OWN CANE POLE

You could use one of those fancy side-scan sonar depthfinders with the new underwater fish-eye orthographic readouts. Or you could go cut a switch of bamboo and do a little cane poling.

If you choose the latter, a decent cane pole is as close as the nearest stand of bamboo. Everyday, ordinary, backyard bamboo works just fine for bream and the occasional small catfish. Make a cane pole our way, with the line anchored to the pole along its entire length, and you'll be able to land anything that doesn't pull you into the pond first.

So there. Drop your line right beside that stump. Sit on a bucket. Doesn't that mud feel squishy between your toes? And, hey, where's your bobber?

STEP 1 Cut a straight piece of cane about 10 feet long. Trim the leaf stems as close as possible. Saw through the fat end at the bottom of a joint so the butt end will have a closed cap. Smooth away the rough edges with some sandpaper.

STEP 2 Tie a string to the slender tip and suspend the cane as it dries to a tan color. (This could take a month or longer.) You can weight it with a brick to help straighten out a curved pole.

STEP 3 With an arbor knot, attach a 20-pound Dacron line a few inches above the place where you hold the rod. Lay the line along the length of the pole and whip-finish the running line to the rod with old fly line at two spots in the middle of the rod—a few feet apart—and at the tip. (If the rod tip breaks, the line will remain attached to the pole.) Attach a 2-foot monofilament leader. Total length of the line from the tip of the rod should be about 14 to 16 feet. Finish with a slip bobber, a split shot, and a long-shank Aberdeen hook for easy removal. —T.E.N.

56 KILL A FISH HUMANELY

The American Veterinary Medical Association's guidelines on euthanasia propose "cranial concussion [stunning] followed by decapitation or pithing [severing or destroying the spinal cord]." It's just five seconds, and you're done—and a better person for it.

STUN The brain of most fish is located behind and slightly above the eye, at about a 10 o'clock position relative to the pupil. Strike there using a short, heavy baton or a rock.

PITH Insert a knife blade into the skull and twist. Or slice just behind the brain to completely sever the spinal cord. —T.E.N.

57 LAND A FISH WITH VELVET GLOVES

Always land fish in very clean water. Think about it: You're on a mud bank, and you're stomping around fighting a fish. The last thing you want to do is drag a tired fish through a bunch of crud. —T.E.N.

58 MASTER THE TUBE JIG

Stream-bred smallmouths are pigs for crayfish, and nothing imitates a craw like a tube jig.

SCENT CONTROL Jam a small piece of sponge soaked with scent into the tube.

DEPTH PERCEPTION In still water, use a 3/4-ounce jighead for water less than 10 feet deep; 1/4-ounce for water 10 to 20 feet deep; and 3/8-ounce for water deeper than 20 feet. Add weight in moving water.

CRAW CRAWL Let the jig fall to the bottom. Reel up the slack and count to 10. Bass will often strike right away. Start a series of rod-tip lifts. The jig should swim a foot off the bottom and then flutter down. —T.E.N.

Nothing imitates crayfish like a crayfish-colored tube jig.

59 CAST LIKE A CHURCH STEEPLE

A steeple cast solves some of the roll cast's deficiencies. It's easier to use with weighted flies or lines, and you can change the direction of your cast midstroke.

But it's not easy. Practice first to prevent unholy language.

STEP 1 Start with the rod tip almost touching the water, and the rod hand rotated away from the body so the reel faces up. Begin with a sidearm backstroke, but rotate at the elbow and then raise the casting arm swiftly vertical. This is an outward and upward motion. With the rod tip directly overhead, the upper arm is at a right angle with your forearm, which is vertical.

STEP 2 Stop the rod abruptly at the 12 o'clock position. The line should be tight and straight overhead.

STEP 3 Make a brisk forward cast, stopping abruptly at the 2 or 3 o'clock position.

—T.E.N.

60 WINTERIZE AN OUTBOARD ENGINE

Here's how to make sure your outboard motor starts up with the first pull come spring—so you can get right down to business.

STEP 1 Add fuel stabilizer to gas, following the manufacturer's directions. Run the motor for 5 to 10 minutes and then disengage the fuel line until the engine dies.

STEP 2 Remove spark plugs and spray fogging oil into each cylinder. Replace spark plugs. Crank the engine to spread the oil.

STEP 3 Change the lower-unit oil. This will remove all the water that might freeze and expand over the winter.

STEP 4 Pull the propeller off and grease the shaft splines. Replace the propeller.

STEP 5 Clear the lower-unit water inlets and speedometer pitot tube of any junk with a pipe cleaner. —T.E.N.

61 RIG A STINGER HOOK

Catch light-biting walleyes with a second hook rigged toward the tail of a live minnow. (This trick puts bait-stealing perch and crappies in the frying pan, too.) Using limp monofilament, tie one end of the stinger line to the bend in the primary hook with an improved clinch knot. Attach the stinger hook—a slightly smaller single hook or a treble—with another improved clinch knot, and embed it either behind the dorsal fin or into the muscle just ahead of the tail. Leave enough line between the two hooks so that the rig will work with baitfish of slightly varying sizes. —T.E.N.

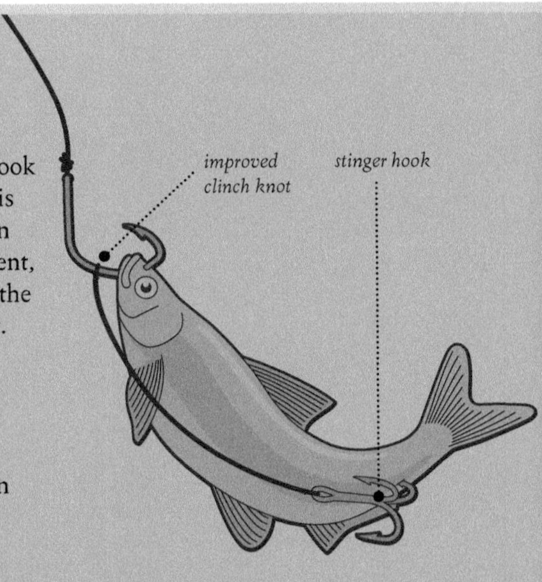

62 READ A TROUT'S TABLE MANNERS

When trying to figure out which fly to cast to a rising trout, most of us will take any help we can get. And in fact, there's help to be had right in front of you: A close look at how a trout is surfacing—its rise form—can speak volumes about what it's eating. Here's a guide to five common rise forms. It's not foolproof, but it will help you catch more fish. —T.E.N.

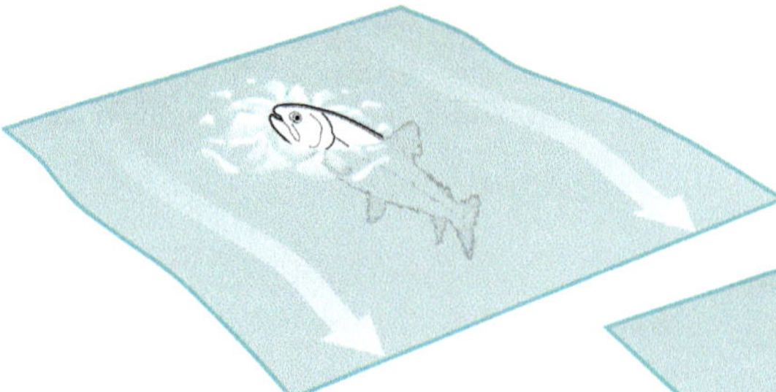

Bulging, splashy rises in fast currents are a good clue to a caddisfly hatch.

If an angler sees a casual, almost slow-motion rise and hears a soft kissing sound, that's a fish taking mayfly spinners in the surface film.

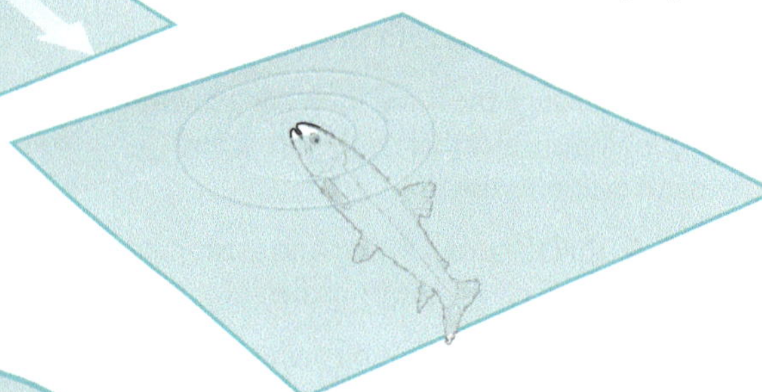

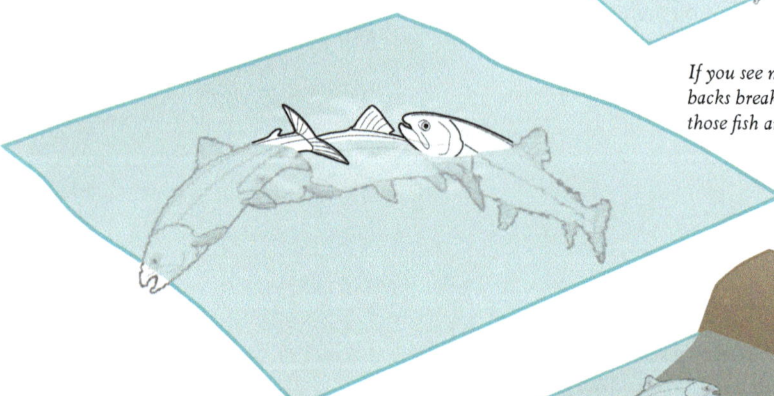

If you see noses and heads and backs breaking the water surface, those fish are taking duns.

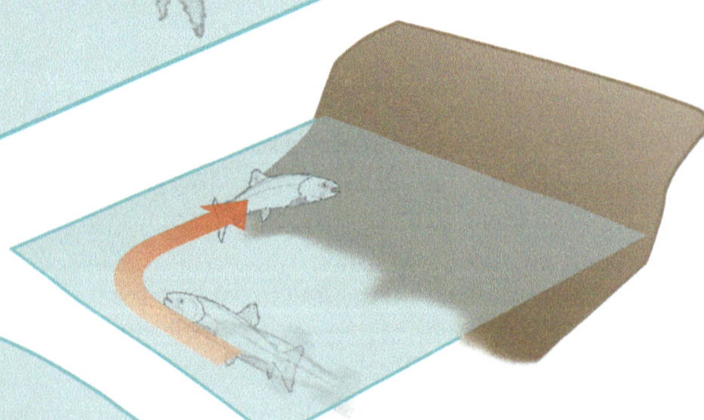

Trout that dart like knives are taking damselfly nymphs, which move very quickly from the water column toward the stream bank.

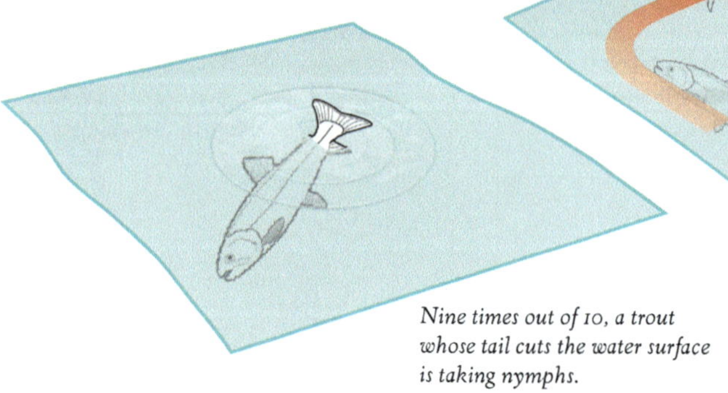

Nine times out of 10, a trout whose tail cuts the water surface is taking nymphs.

63 MAKE A QUICK-SINKING FLY LINE

Fast-sinking fly lines are the bomb for catching shad surging up spring-swollen rivers, and they're deadly on striped bass, too. They're a cinch to build out of a few inexpensive materials and the leftover fly line that lies snarled on your workbench. For this, use LC-13, a lead-core line that weighs 13 grains per foot.

START SNIPPING (These are directions for a 9-wt line; experiment with lengths of lead-core for other line weights): Cut off the running line section of an old fly line. Cut a 28-foot section of LC-13. Cut a 6-inch length of 30-pound braided monofilament running line.

BRING ON THE KNOTS Attach backing to one end of the running line with a nail knot. Then insert the free tip of the running line into one end of the braided mono. Next, work the running line into the braided mono almost halfway by grasping the braided mono between thumb and forefinger of one hand and pushing toward it with the thumb and forefinger of the other hand, creating a bellows-like accordion.

FINISH Repeat above with one end of the LC-13. Tie a whip finish to the two ends of the braided mono sleeve and apply a few drops of pliable glue. Finally, tie in a loop—commercial or homemade with 40-pound mono—directly to the end of the sinking line. You're ready to dredge. —T.E.N.

64 HAUL-CAST A FLY 60 FEET OR MORE

If you can tug on a fly line, you can learn to do the single and double haul. The trick is timing. The key is practice.

Grab the fly line close to the rod with your line hand. Start your back cast. Just as you begin your backward power stroke, pull the line (in your line hand) toward your hip pocket. Don't jerk—just make a smooth, fast motion of a foot and a half or so and release. Your back cast should shoot rearward with added zip. That's a single haul—and often all you need for a little extra distance.

To complete the double haul, start by easing your line hand back toward the reel as your back cast unfurls.

Then, just as you begin your forward power stroke, pull downward again as before. Finish the cast and let the slack line shoot through your hand. —K.M.

65 TIE THIS FLY IF IT'S THE LAST THING YOU DO

The Clouser Minnow has joined the likes of Woolly Buggers and Muddlers as a global standard among fly patterns. Unlike the others, though, Clousers are easily made by novice fly-tying fishermen. The fly's jigging action works great for everything from crappies and brown trout to striped bass and redfish (Lefty Kreh has landed 86 different species on it). Vary the fly size and color to suit your quarry.

For this example, you'll need a medium-shank-length streamer hook, some nylon or polyester size 3/0 thread, some dumbbell-style eyes, natural white plus dyed chartreuse bucktail, and some Flashabou or similar material. Use clear nail polish as a fly-tying cement. Here's how to put it all together. —J.M.

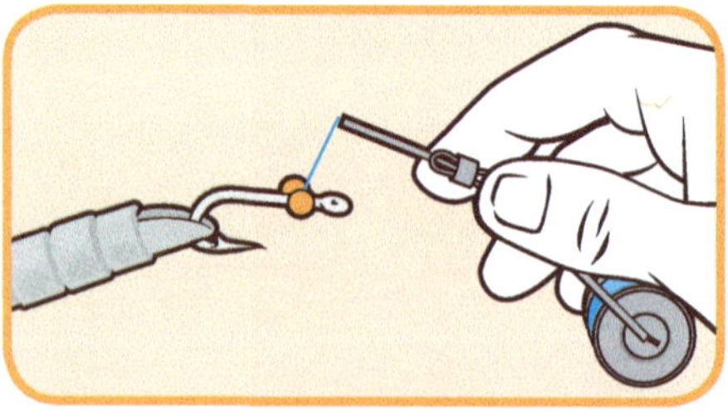

STEP 1 With the hook in a tying vise, secure the thread one-third of the shank length back from the hook eye. Tie dumbbell eyes securely on top of the shank with figure-eight thread wraps. Add a small dab of cement to the wraps.

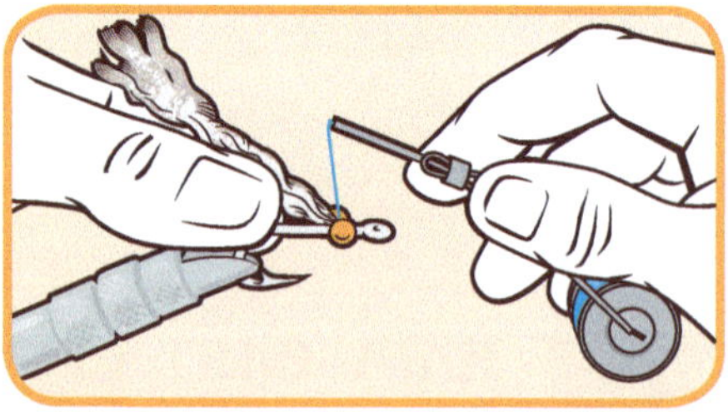

STEP 2 Tie in a sparse bunch of white bucktail behind the hook eye and in front of the eyes. Wind the thread to a position right behind the eyes. Pull the white bucktail firmly into the groove between the eyes, and tie it down again right behind the eyes.

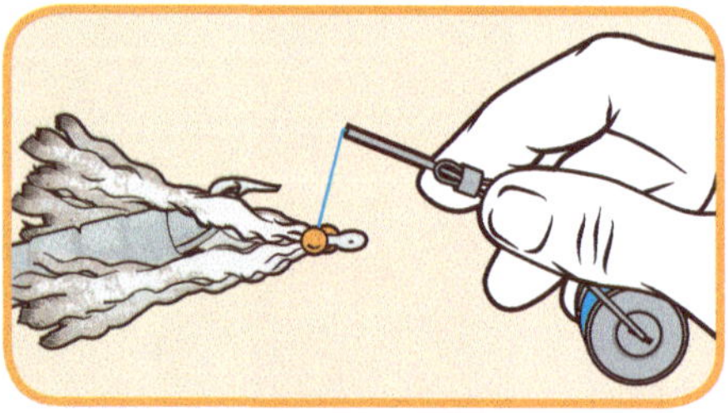

STEP 3 Turn the hook over in the vise so that the hook point is up. Add about six strands of Flashabou or a similar material.

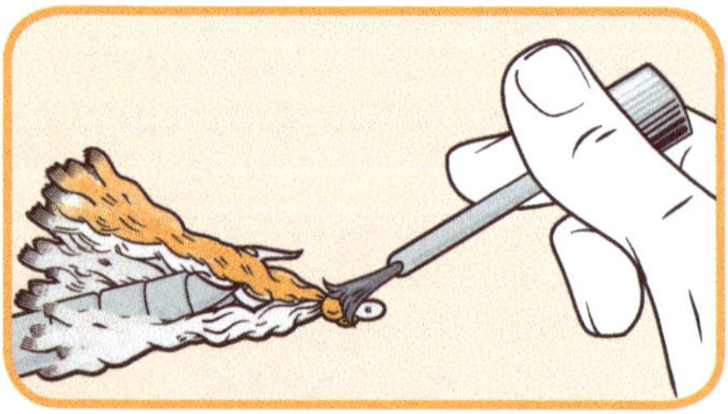

STEP 4 Tie in a bunch of chartreuse bucktail, and build a neat conical head with thread wraps, finishing with two half hitches. Coat the finished fly head with nail polish (two coats). —J.M.

66 MAKE A QUICK-SINKING FLY LINE

Had their captains backed the *Dartmouth*, *Beaver*, and *Eleanor* into their respective slips, the Brits might have been able to goose the engines and leave the Boston Tea Party rebels flatfooted on the dock. Moral of the story: There are lots of reasons to know how to back a boat into a slip. (Practice in a quiet cove to learn which way your bow turns when you attempt to back in a straight line—a phenomenon known as "propeller walk.")

STEP 1 Idle to your target slip. As your bow reaches the slip just before yours, stop forward motion by bumping into reverse. Shift into neutral and turn the wheel away from your slip as far as it will turn.

STEP 2 Bump the throttle into forward to start a pivot turn. Shift to neutral, turn the steering wheel in the opposite direction, and then bump into reverse. This will stop the pivot.

STEP 3 Align the transom with the slip, and back in slowly. Remember which direction your bow wants to "walk" when moving in reverse. Adjust course by bumping the drive into and out of gear.
—T.E.N.

67 CRIPPLE A FLY FOR AN IRRESISTIBLE TREAT

Heavily fished trout often require triggers in your fly pattern to prompt a strike. Many fish will key on malformed or wingless duns or crippled flies—put a fly out there with beautiful tails or upright wings, and they won't even look at it. That means you need to go with a pattern of trailing shucks. And get creative. Cut the wings off flies. Trim them so they fall over on one side. Most anglers can't bring themselves to take scissors to a perfectly good fly, but not every fish is a perfectionist. —T.E.N.

68 PADDLE A CANOE INTO A GALE

The right way seems wrong: Trim the canoe slightly bow heavy to keep it heading into the wind. Kneel in the bottom of the boat and use short, quick strokes. Feather the paddle on your return stroke, turning the blade parallel to the water surface so it won't catch the wind. Keep the boat pointed into the waves and use every bit of windbreak possible—even distant land points can provide relief from wind and swell. —T.E.N.

69 DRESS A FLY CORRECTLY

It's easy to destroy a fly's profile by smashing and grinding in floatant. Here's the lowdown on the correct way to make your fly float.

Grasp the hook point between your thumb and index finger. Place one drop of floatant directly on the top of the hackle fibers. Instead of applying the floatant to your fingers and then working it into the fly, use a finger on your other hand to flick the floatant into the fly materials. —T.E.N.

70 RUN A RAPID

Learning to negotiate a straight-on ledge drop or chute of water between two rocks is a basic skill of Whitewater Canoeing 101.

SCOUT IT OUT First, get a good look at what you're getting into. It's best to scout from shore because looking at a piece of moving water from the side gives you an entirely different perspective.

Make sure it's what you expect—no rocks or drops you won't be able to see from the water. Find the V of water that flushes through the rapid cleanly, with a series of standing waves at the bottom that are a sign of clear deep water. Be sure that you plan how to avoid curling waves formed by underwater rocks and souse holes.

PREPARE TO PROCEED Next, move into position slowly. That way, you can escape if you have a last-second change of mind. Set up the approach without a lot of power until you establish your line.

COMMIT YOURSELF Once you've done all of your preparation, it's commitment time. Get yourself correctly lined up, and just start powering forward. Be aware that the forward stroke is the simplest means of bracing a canoe in turbulent water, so the best thing to do is to keep paddling. That will also prevent you from committing the worst rapids-running mistake: grabbing the gunwale.

—T.E.N.

71 FILLET THE BONIEST FISH THAT SWIMS

The Y-bones embedded in the dorsal flesh of a northern pike prevent many anglers from dining on one of the tastiest fish around. Learn to remove them, and you will never curse when a 3-pound pike bashes your walleye rig.

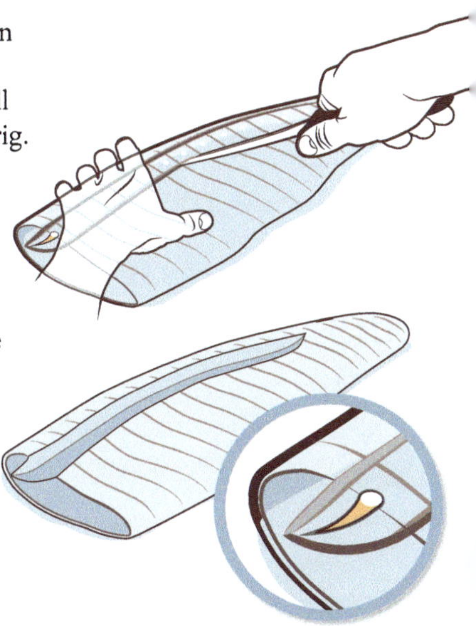

STEP 1 Fillet the fish, removing flesh from the ribs as you would with any other fish.

STEP 2 Find the row of white dots visible midway between the spine and the top of the fillet. These are the tips of the Y-bones. Slice along the top of these dots, nearly through the fillet, following the curve of the bones.

STEP 3 Next, you'll want to slice along the bottom of the Y-bones, following their shape, while aiming the knife tip toward the first incision.

STEP 4 Connect the two cuts above the fish's anus. Remove the bony strip. Get the grease popping.

—T.E.N.

72 FLY CAST IN CIRCLES

When brush or high ground limits your back cast, break the rules with a lob cast.

STEP 1 Strip the line in so you have the leader and about 10 feet of line in the water. Point the rod at the fly and then pick it all up, right out of the water at once, and make a big, fast, clockwise, circular pass overhead. The reel should actually move in a half-circular motion up above your head.

STEP 2 Stop the rod behind at the position where you would stop a traditional back cast, feel it load, and then fire all the line out with one forward shot. You can seriously launch a heavy fly or sink-tip line this way. —T.E.N.

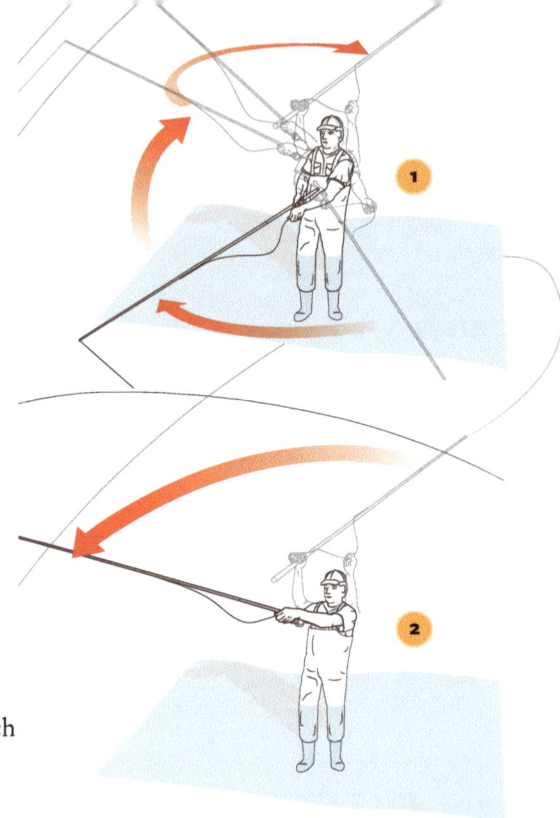

73 LAND BIG TROUT SOLO

A 20-inch trout on the line and no one to marvel at your fishing skills? First things first. You can't gloat until you get the fish in, so here's how to land a brag-worthy trout all by your lonesome.

STEP 1 Start with your rod overhead, and with 10 feet of line out. Next, rotate your rod arm to move the rod to a horizontal plane, making sure that it's pointing upstream, and keeping the pressure on the fish.

STEP 2 Back up toward the bank, steering the fish toward shore.

STEP 3 Raise the rod back overhead to vertical. Drop your net and scoop the fish under its chin. —T.E.N.

74 TURN A KID ON TO FLYFISHING

Schooling kids on flyfishing doesn't have to be as trying as helping them with their math homework. Start by limiting the time on the pond to a half-hour chunk. That prevents the kid from getting frustrated and the teacher from blowing a fuse.

Here's how to optimize those minutes.

KNOW YOUR STUDENTS Tailor your comments to kids' age levels. A 10-year-old might understand what you mean by "feel the rod load," but a 6-year-old won't. Remember to bring your own rod so you don't take the rod from the kid; that feels like punishment. Don't wait for perfection. Instead, introduce new concepts quickly to battle boredom.

TEACH TIMING Start off with sidearm casts so that the kids can watch the fly line and better understand the physics of casting. Emphasize that fly casting is about timing, not strength.

MAKE A CASTING CALL Tell the kids to treat the rod like a ringing telephone: Bring the rod up close to their ear, say, "Hello, this is Drew Smith," and then set the "phone" down. That's the basic fly-casting movement: Sweep the rod back, stop it, let the rod load, and then make a forward cast.

KEEP THINGS ROLLING If the kids struggle with the basics, switch to roll casting for the time being. It's easier to learn, and will help build their confidence. With a bit of success, they'll be ready to move forward and tackle the next step: a standard cast.

TIME TO FISH Find a likely spot: Choose a time and place where the fish are willing. Bream beds are perfect.

GO PRO Do the kids bristle at every suggestion you make? Sign up for a casting school, or hire a guide for a half day and outsource the tricky parts.

CHOOSE A ROD A soft action helps kids feel the rod flex and load. Be wary of supershort rods, which can be difficult to cast. Go for an 8-foot, 6-weight, two-piece outfit.

CONSIDER LINE WEIGHT Overline the rod by one line weight to help with easier turnover.

GO EASY WITH FLIES Get a barbed fly stuck in the child's forehead and you can forget about him or her as a future fishing buddy. Only use flies with barbless hooks. For practice, tie orange egg yarn next to the fly to make it visible. On the water, cast big high-floating flies like Stimulators.

—T.E.N.

75 SUPERCHARGE SALMON EGG BEADS

Beads resembling eggs are the fly patterns of choice wherever trout, char, and steelhead follow spawning salmon. Unaltered beads will draw strikes right out of the package, but you can make them more effective by applying a realistic finish and softer texture, so the fish won't spit them out before you can set the hook.

STEP 1 Stick one end of a toothpick through the hole in the bead to use as a handle. Paint the entire bead with fingernail polish (something sheer or clear). Stick the toothpick upright into a block of Styrofoam and let dry one hour.

STEP 2 Pour some soft epoxy into a bowl and roll the bead in it, coating all sides. Stick the toothpick back into the Styrofoam in a horizontal position. The epoxy will gather more heavily on the bottom side, so the bead will be slightly out of round after drying. Dry overnight.

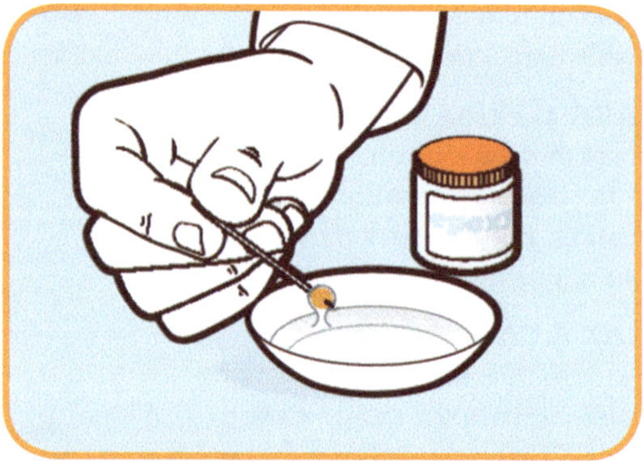

STEP 3 To rig, slip a bead onto your tippet, and then pass the end of the tippet back around and through the bead again, forming a loop. Pass the end of the tippet through the loop and cinch tight to secure the bead. Tie on a hook with an upturned eye to the tippet 1 to 3 inches from the bead. With the bead secured above the hook, it will look and drift more naturally, and the fish you catch will be hooked on the outside of the jaw. Fish this under a strike indicator.

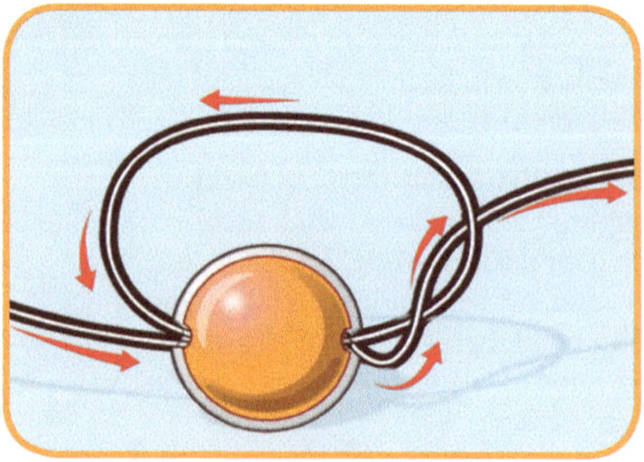

NOTE It is against regulations to use a bare-bead, bare-hook combination in some fly-only waters. Check before you try this tip.

Match the beads you use to the size of eggs drifting in the river: 6mm for sockeye salmon, 8mm for coho, 10mm for kings. Fish may choose older-looking eggs over "fresh" ones, so stock up on a few different colors.

—K.M.

76 TAKE THE FIGHT TO THE FISH IN SMALL WATER

Big fish are so strong and tough in tight quarters. Two things are crucial to landing monster fish in small rivers. First, as soon as you know the fish is hooked well, go to the head of the pool. Put some distance between the rod and whatever rapids and logs and rocks are jumbled up in the tailout. Second, once you have some room, it's critical to make the fish go through at least two runs against the drag. Don't be afraid to wave your arms above the water if you have to. You simply must get the fish to work and tire out.

Instead of fighting with the rod held straight up and down, turn it at a 45-degree angle, and sweep the tip to the left or right to lead the fish into the current or into deep runs. You may need to steer a big fish into shallow water so it will get nervous and make a break for the current. If it just sits in the stream, holding, do something to get it moving again. Take control of the action. —T.E.N.

77 TRAILER A BOAT IN A HEAVY WIND

If you have to load your boat in a vicious crosswind, follow these steps for success.

STEP 1 Don't back your trailer too deeply into the water. You need to maintain firm contact between the hull and the bottom bunks.

STEP 2 Steer into the wind for control.

STEP 3 Approach the trailer at as close to a 90-degree angle as you can get, given ramp design. As you near the imaginary line that extends backward from the trailer, turn slightly toward the trailer. The wind will catch the bow and move it toward a centered line with the trailer. Bump up the throttle so the bow enters the back of the trailer at an angle pointing slightly into the wind. Momentum will carry the boat into a straight line.

STEP 4 Apply enough power to push the bow eye to within 6 to 8 inches of the bow stop. Check your centering. Take a bow. —T.E.N.

78 SET ANY ANCHOR, ANYTIME

Head upwind or upcurrent and then lower the anchor all the way to the bottom. Anchors grab best when they first lie down. Reverse the engine and slowly back away to a distance of 7 to 10 times the depth of the water. —T.E.N.

river anchors for moving water

mushrooms for lakes

fluke hooks for sandy coastal waters

79 CATCH BAIT WITH A SABIKI RIG

Sabiki rigs are ready-to-fish dropper lines festooned with small hooks trimmed with reflective materials and sometimes bucktail. These rigs are great for catching marine baitfish, but freshwater baits like white perch and small bream will suck in the hooks too. (Check local regulations before using.)

When fishing in freshwater, you're going to want to go for the smallest hooks you can find. Attach a 1- or 2-ounce weight, and jig slowly up and down with a long rod over likely structure. Don't make the mistake of bringing it in with the first strike. A hooked fish will move the hooks around and actually help with attracting other fish.

To store your sabiki rig, wrap the rig around a wine cork, sticking each hook into the cork as you wrap. —T.E.N.

80 WIN THE TOUGHEST FISH FIGHT

Occasionally, when it all comes together, a true behemoth will suck in your lure. What you do next is the difference between glory and another "almost" story.

KNOW YOUR KNOT WILL HOLD Most big fish are lost due to failed knots. Wet each knot with saliva before cinching it tight, and make sure you seat it properly. If you are less than 100 percent confident in the knot you just tied, take the time to retie it. Every time.

CLEAR THE COVER Bruiser fish will quickly burrow into weeds or head for a snag, so establish authority as soon as you set the hook. Resist the temptation to hoot, holler, and point. Put pressure on immediately and keep your rod tip up. Don't force the action but steer the fish into the clear.

TURN AND BURN Once the fish is in open water, let it wear down. As the fish moves, bend the rod away from the direction in which it's swimming and lower the rod to tighten the angle. Don't winch it; you simply want to turn the head and guide the fish in a different direction, burning energy all the way.

DON'T CHOKE The few seconds after your first boat-side glimpse of a bona fide monster are critical. If you can see him, he can see you. Prepare for a last-ditch escape maneuver. Be ready to jab the rod tip into the water if the fish dives under the boat. Don't grab the line. Stay focused on keeping the fish off-balance until he's in the boat. If you're using a net, make sure you lead the fish in headfirst. —T.E.N.

81 CROSS A SWOLLEN CREEK OR (SLIGHTLY) RAGING RIVER

Look before you leap. Current moves most swiftly where a stream narrows, so try crossing at a wider, shallower spot. Scout the far shore to make sure you can clamber to safety—no slick mudbanks or bluffs. Unhook hip belts and loosen shoulder straps on packs in case you need to jettison your load before going into the drink. Cut a shoulder-high staff or break out the trekking poles and remove your socks and insoles. Wet shoes are easier to tolerate than wet everything. Lace your boots firmly and then cross the stream diagonally, moving sideways like a crab and slightly downstream, yielding to the current. Nice and easy keeps you upright. Move only one point of contact at a time: Plant your staff, take a step, plant your staff, take another. —K.M.

82 PLANT A CRAPPIE TREE

Crappies crave structure, and a PVC tree will attract slabs to the most barren lake bottom. The slick pipes keep hangups to a minimum.

THE TRUNK Drill a small hole through one end of a 4-inch-diameter PVC pipe. (The pipe length depends somewhat on the depth of its final destination. A 4- to 5-foot tree works well.) Next, drill three ¾-inch holes along each side of the pipe "trunk" at angles so the "branches" will angle upward and shed hooks easily. Insert a long nail into the small hole you drilled at the bottom of the trunk and anchor it in a 3-gallon flowerpot with concrete.

THE BRANCHES Cut six 3-foot lengths of ¾-inch PVC pipe for your branches. Drill a small hole through the end of two of these. Insert the PVC branches into the holes in the trunk, securing them with PVC glue. —T.E.N.

PVC may not register on many fish finders, so mark your tree's location on your GPS.

To attract crappies, fill two empty 20-ounce water bottles—punched with small holes—with dry dog food and cap the bottles tightly. Tie these to the branches that have the small holes.

83 RIG LEAD-CORE LINES FOR THE DEEPEST LUNKERS

Knowing how to troll with metered lead-core lines is indispensable for many big-lake fisheries, where the majority of anglers pull lead-core lines from fall to ice-up. These lines are metered in colors, and each color is 30 feet long. Use 18-pound lead core in a splice-in rig to get lures down deep and defeat the lack of sensitivity that comes with heavy sinkers. Here's how:

STEP 1 Spool up 200 to 300 feet of 14- or 20-pound monofilament backing. Tie on a No. 18 barrel swivel with an improved clinch knot.

STEP 2 Peel back the Dacron sheath from the last 4 to 5 inches of lead-core line and pinch off the lead. This leaves a length of sheath that you can tie onto the barrel swivel with an improved clinch knot.

Wind three colors of lead onto the reel. Peel back another length of sheath, pinch off the lead, and tie on another No. 18 barrel swivel.

STEP 3 Attach to the barrel swivel 50 feet of 10-pound-test fluorocarbon line, then a ball-bearing snap-swivel or plain plug snap, and then the crankbait. —T.E.N.

84 CATCH TROUT AND BASS WITH YOUR ELK

The hide of one bull elk will produce enough hair for 984,376 flies—give or take. So follow these simple steps, and don't let it go to waste.

STEP 1 Cut 6-inch squares of hide. Flesh with a knife blade by removing as much fat and meat as possible without slicing through the roots of the hair.

STEP 2 Salt each square with 1⁄4 cup of salt, rubbing the salt into the flesh side of the hide with your fingers. Let it sit for eight hours, shake off the wet salt, and repeat.

STEP 3 Hang the squares from the game pole and air-dry until it's time to break camp. To get them home, store in an air-permeable bag, such as a pillowcase.

STEP 4 Think outside the caddis box. Sure, elk hair is perfect for caddis imitations. But use your hide for other dry flies such as Humpys and Stimulators; for nymphs such as little yellow stoneflies; and for terrestrials like the Henry's Fork Hopper. Elk hair, because it is a little coarser than deer hair, floats higher, so you can even use it for poppers and bass bugs. —T.E.N.

FIELD & STREAM-APPROVED KNOT #5

85 TIE A CLOVE HITCH

The clove hitch is Boating 101—good for a temporary stay to dock or piling. It's also the foundational knot for many pole-lashing techniques, which may be useful if you don't tie it correctly the first time, your boat drifts away, and you have to lash a long pole together to snag it back. —T.E.N.

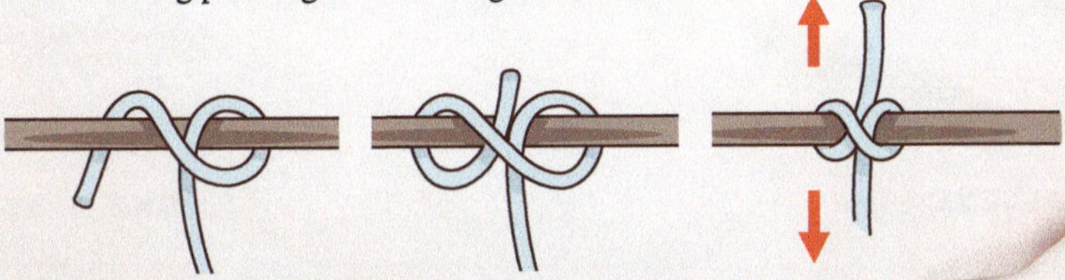

86 CHOOSE THE RIGHT BASS LURE

Bass lures can be divided into five broad categories depending on the lure's design and how the angler manipulates the bait. Pack a tackle box with a few lures from each of these categories, and you'll catch bass in any weather, from any water. —T.E.N.

SURFACE LURE Otherwise known as topwater lures, these hard-bodied baits kick up a fuss. They gurgle, pop, jerk, waddle, and dart across the water surface and can draw explosive strikes from hungry bass. Surface lures with a cupped face are known as "poppers," and pop and spray water as the angler snaps the rod tip. Poppers can imitate anything from dying baitfish to frantic frogs. Thin, lightweight "pencil poppers" skitter like a minnow on its last legs—and few bass will turn down such an easy meal. One of the best retrieves for cigar-shaped surface lures is called "walking the dog," in which the lure glides back and forth with a zigzag action as the angler twitches the rod tip low to the water.

SPINNERBAIT Safety-pin style spinnerbaits look nothing like a natural food—but they catch bass like crazy. Built on a V-shaped wire frame, the baits have one or more revolving blades threaded to one wire shaft, while the other is tipped with a weighted hook dressed with an often garish skirt of brightly colored rubber or silicone. The spinning blades produce flash and vibration, while the wild, undulating rubber skirts—often glittering with metal flakes—give bass a temptation they often can't resist. Depending on the rate of retrieve, spinnerbaits can be skittered across the water's surface, helicoptered straight down through the water column, or bumped along the bottom. Many anglers consider spinners "search baits," because they allow you to cover lots of water fast and help you figure out where bass are holding in short order.

THE ONE LURE YOU NEED FOR ...

WALLEYE *grub lure*

PIKE *spoon lure*

SMALLMOUTH *grub lure*

SOFT PLASTIC Few baits have changed the fishing world as much as soft plastics. Introduced as a large worm imitation in 1951, the realistic, lifelike baits now come in a dizzying array of shapes—worms, salamanders, baitfish, crayfish, snakes, slugs, frogs, lizards, mice, and more. Fishing tactics for soft plastics are just as varied. Many are threaded on to a lead jig. Others are rigged with no weight on a weedless, wide-gap hook. And some of the most popular soft plastics are among the most pungent—many of these baits are manufactured with natural or artificial scents and oils that prompt bass to chow down. If you ever feel overwhelmed by soft-plastic selections, it's hard to go wrong with a purple or black worm slow-twitched across the bottom.

CRANK BAIT These hard-bodied diving lures imitate a wide range of tantalizing fish foods, most often baitfish such as shad or bluegill, but they can also imitate crayfish when worked right off the bottom. Made of wood or plastic and clad in realistic paints and holographic finishes, most crankbaits sport a hard plastic lip that forces them to dive and wobble when "cranked" through bass water. Crankbaits come in shallow, medium, and deep-diving versions, depending on the size of the plastic diving bill.

STICKBAIT Imitating everything from long, slender minnows to full-grown trout, stickbaits are most often fished with a twitching, stop-and-start motion that looks like prey species darting in and out of cover, or an injured and crippled baitfish struggling to stay alive. That herky-jerky death dance action spawns vicious strikes by feeding bass and can coax even the most close-mouthed largemouth to open wide. Many stickbaits come in a jointed version for even more emphatic action.

PANFISH *mini-tube*

TROUT *in-line spinner*

STRIPER *stickbait*

87 SURVIVE TROUT MADNESS

I wake to the sound of a tent door zipper. Scott Wood is ready to roar at 5:15 a.m., the Rocky Tangle's torture seemingly forgotten. But I feel like 40 miles of bad road. I pull the sleeping bag over my head and curl my body around knobs of rock and tussocks of blueberries.

In just five minutes, though, I'm climbing into cold waders. As the sun winks through spruce trees, we pick our way across a ledge drop at the bottom of the Rocky Tangle. Fog rises from a slot of water maybe 20 feet by 40 feet.

It's the swiftest, deepest run we've seen in three days. My hands are shaking, but I'm not sure if it's from the cold or from nervous anticipation. Months of planning and logistical troubles have led us here. If this river holds scads of big fish, this is exactly the kind of place they'll be—stacked up in pools as they nose upstream during prespawn runs.

It doesn't take long.

David Falkowski drops a fly into the water first, rips it cross-current, and hangs on as his rod bends double, like a diviner's stick pointing the way to the mother lode. "Three pounds, maybe. Not bad," he hollers as the fish comes to hand.

"Of course," he adds, "it's the largest brook trout I've ever seen in my life!"

In less than 60 seconds, each of us is into a brookie. We catch fish with 60-foot casts and we catch them six feet from the canoe. Hooked trout run between our legs. One takes Bill Mulvey's fly as he merely dabbles it into the water at his feet, wetting the marabou before making a real cast. Twice I catch a bragging-sized brookie while walking from pool to pool, dragging my fly behind me.

They are cookie-cutter characters, four-pounder after five-pounder after four-pounder again, and none of us complain. The females are hammered from verdigris and brass, swollen with roe. And the gaudy, prespawn males have the appearance of a brook trout with its tail stuck in an electric socket. Many are slashed with scars from close calls with toothy pike.

In an hour and a half, we catch 32 brook trout, two and a half to six pounds apiece. They hit the traditional northern speckle fare—Mickey Finns and Woolly Buggers, Stimulators and Sofa Pillows, streamers up to six inches long. They knock deerhair mice out of the water. But that's not all. One of my most effective flies is a chartreuse surf candy I tied for saltwater false albacore. We catch them on bass bugs, bream poppers, and silverside streamers. It's the fishing we came for, but not a one of us really thought we'd find.

In fact, none of us could have dreamed of the amazing, improbable day about to unfold. Twice more we haul the canoes and gear over shallow, rocky outlets, and twice more we pound swiftwater outfall pools that seem to boast a 50-50 water-to-fish ratio. That night we collapse on the rocky shore of an unnamed lake and watch the northern lights arc overhead like a lava lamp stretched from horizon to horizon. Mars is up, and Bill swears he hears wolves howling. Scott and David stick their heads out the tent door to catch the sound, but I crawl into my sleeping bag to count the blue-haloed dots on the shimmering flanks of the brook trout that swim through my dreams.

—T. Edward Nickens, *Field & Stream*, "Quest for the Mother Lode," April 2004

88 CATCH KILLER BROWNS

Just about every trout stream has them—huge, predatory brown trout that fishermen rarely see and hardly ever catch. Few fishermen are as dialed in to the nuances of catching large brown trout as Michigan guide Ray Schmidt. For 45 years, Schmidt has been chasing browns in the waters where the species was initially introduced to the United States. Schmidt's biggest Michigan brown is a 26-incher, taken on a streamer at night next to a logjam. Schmidt says that most anglers have no clue what really lurks below the surface of their favorite trout stream. At the right time—usually night—that gentle, meandering river can radically transform into a veritable "killing field" for predatory browns. "These large browns sometimes go on the hunt for food, traveling a mile or two each night in search of prey," says Schmidt. "This is a predator that eats mice, baby ducks, and other creatures in, on, or around the water." In other words, if you want to catch large, you have to fish large, and usually in low-light conditions.

Summer is a particularly opportune time to fish for big nighttime browns. The warm water increases trout metabolism, meaning they must eat more. And these big predators will go on the hunt when the waters cool down at night. —K.D.

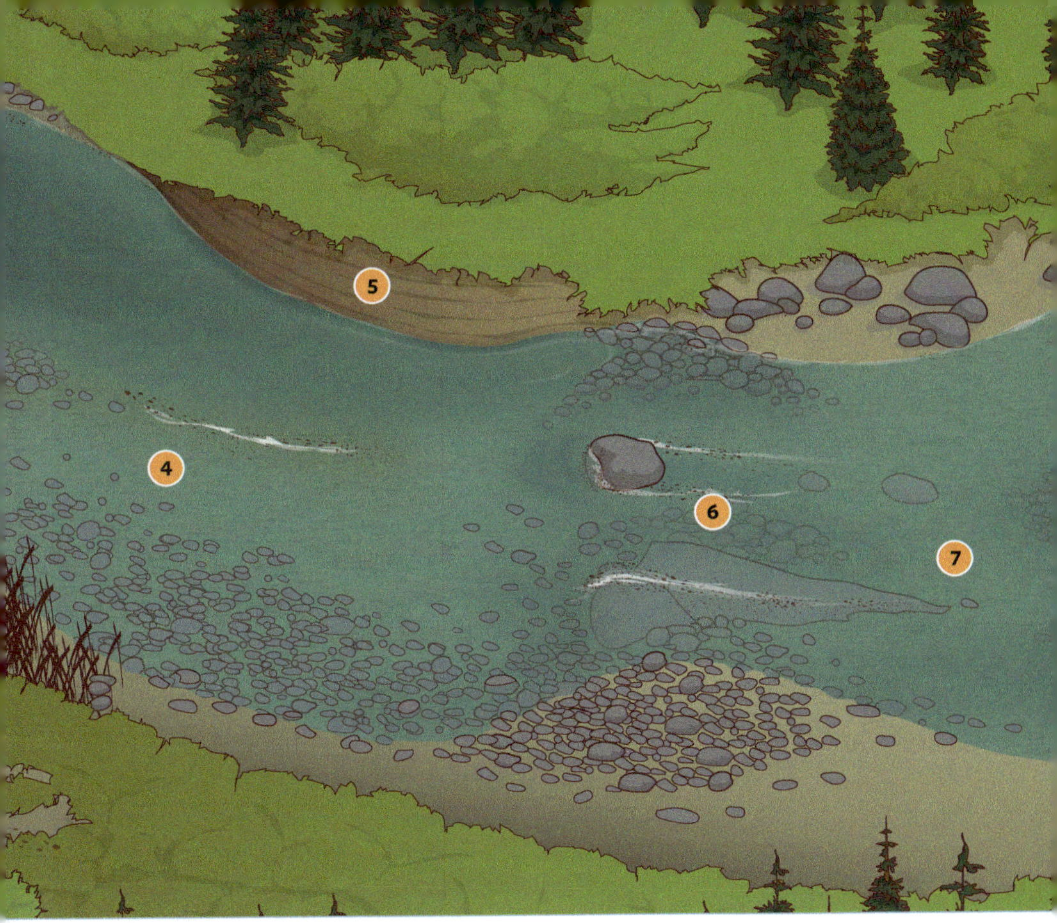

1 SHUN THE RIFFLE
Sure, riffles typically hold trout—rainbows. When you're stalking big browns, you want to avoid the water where smaller fish will seize the opportunity to take your bait or fly. If you're looking for a trophy brown, they're distractions.

2 SCOUT AND LISTEN
Some of your most productive time may be spent on a high bank. Learn to recognize the sound that a brown trout makes as it gulps something from the surface. And watch for subtle disturbances in current lines.

3 FIND THE LION'S DEN
Large brown trout thrive in river runs with three ingredients: depth, cover, and slow and steady current. Find the spot in the river where currents and obstructions have scoured a deep hole.

4 FOLLOW THE BUBBLES
Look for seams where fast currents meet slow or where deep water meets shallow currents. Cast into the bubble line created on the surface. Memorize these locations and fish them at night.

5 CASE THE BANK
Big browns will often lurk in the shadows of undercut banks, where they are protected from their predators but can easily dart out and inhale a baitfish or a grasshopper. Fish tight to the bank to catch them.

6 TARGET THE CUSHION
Large browns frequently ride the hydraulics in front of a large rock or tree stump in the river. You want to cast both in front of that rock or stump and into the deep scour behind it.

7 FISH MARGINAL WATER
The biggest browns are hardy fish that can thrive in waters often overlooked by most trout anglers. Don't hesitate to fish downstream from the "prime" section of your favorite trout river.

89 LAY YOUR HANDS ON A RIVER MONSTER

There are a number of ways to get your hands on a really big catfish. Noodling expert Gerald Moore places casket-shaped catfish boxes—with a hole the size of a football in one end—in chest-deep water.

On the other hand, some hand-grabbers seed their favorite waters with old water heaters modified for fish. After a few months, a three-person team returns to the box and takes the following steps.

STEP 1 The "checker" assists by blocking the hole with his feet and checking for a fish with a 7-foot pole.

STEP 2 A "helper" stands on the box and helps to steady the checker. Meanwhile, the "grabber" goes underwater and sticks his right arm in the box, up to the elbow to grab the fish.

STEP 3 If the fish bites, he will get all four fingers in the pocket behind its teeth, with his thumb on the outside, then pull it out and wrap it with his left arm. —T.E.N.

90 DOCUMENT A TROPHY FOR A RIGHTEOUS REPLICA

When you catch a memorable fish, you'll want to preserve the memory. Here's how to record the details for your own wall-worthy replica.

MEASURE Always carry a measuring board at least 25 inches long—larger than many standard bass boards. (Saltwater fishing boards work great.) Dunk it in the water before laying out the fish. Measure from the tip of the mouth to the tip of the compressed tail. Gently lift the midsection and measure girth at the widest point. Weigh with a digital scale.

PHOTOGRAPH Take photos of each side, the top of the fish, and the belly. Then switch the camera to "macro" mode and take close-ups of the cheeks, top of the head, and lateral stripe patterns. Make sure to capture any distinctive markings the fish may have.

RECORD Make notes about where you caught the fish. Fish that spend a lot of time in deeper water tend to have light colors; the reverse is true for shallow-water bass. Your detailed notes will help the taxidermist work up the right palette. —T.E.N.

91 TARGET DEEP WATER FOR PIG BASS

Underwater points, submerged roads, old pond dams—deep-water structure holds bass, but many anglers aren't used to probing 30 and 40 feet down. Here's how.

SCHOOL DAZE Once you locate fish, analyze the fish finder to figure out whether they are hanging on top of the hump, to the left or right of the ridge, or off the face of the point as it plunges. A lot of anglers see fish on the fish finder and turn off their brains. Figure out exactly how the fish are using the structure.

MARK THE FISH Idle 50 feet past the school (75 feet in a headwind) and drop a marker buoy (a).

ANCHOR AWEIGH Circle around to the right or left, always staying about two-thirds of your maximum casting distance away from the school.

In calm conditions, drop anchor (b) when you are even with the marker buoy and then back down until you are even with the school. In a wind, continue past the marker buoy before dropping anchor (c) and drift down until you are even with the school.

MAKE THE CAST Think before you cast. Don't throw right at the fish; by the time your lure reaches the target depth, it will be halfway back to the boat. Instead, throw your bait beyond the fish (d) as far as you can and let the lure sink. Now you're placing the bait right in the strike zone. As for gear, go no lighter than a 7-foot heavy-action rod. Deep water means dealing with serious line stretch, and a long stiff rod results in better hooksets. —T.E.N.

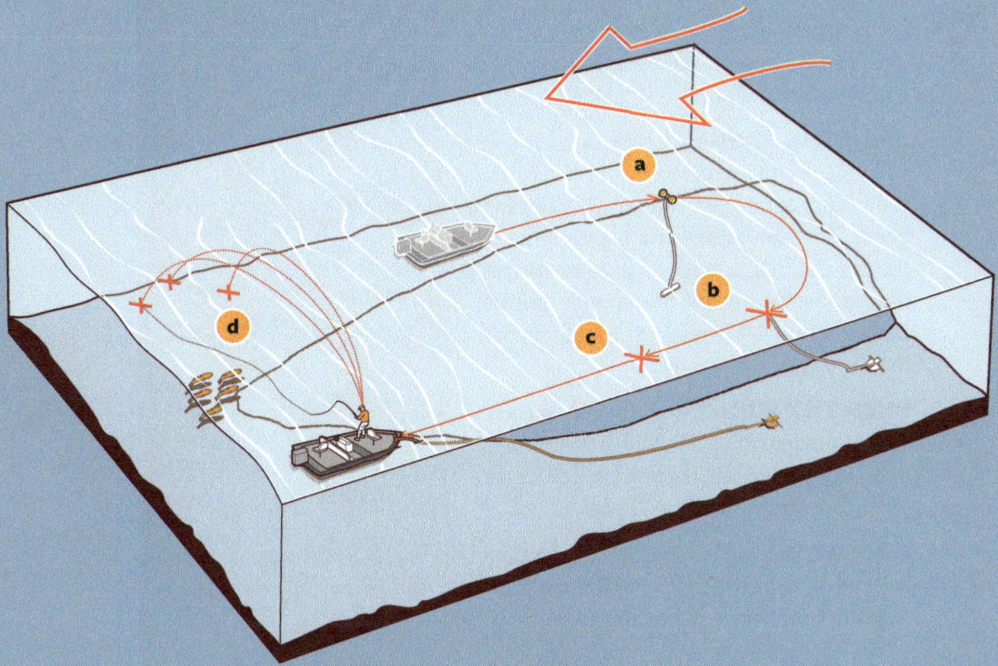

92 FLY CAST FROM A KAYAK

Casting from a kayak will test the skills of even the best fly angler. Here's how to modify your style for the confines of a sit-on-top.

MIND YOUR LINE The tall sides of a traditional stripping basket don't cut it when you're casting from a seated position, but you need something to keep your fly line from tangling. A cheap 9 x 11-inch baking pan works as a makeshift stripping basket.

OVERLINE YOUR ROD Using a line weight one step up from the weight of a fly rod will add distance and cut down on false casts.

CUSTOMIZE YOUR CAST Keep your back cast out of the water. To begin, hold your rod arm farther in front of your body than normal to move the power stroke forward of the stopping position on the back cast. Start with the rod tip low and with zero slack in the line, accelerate smoothly, and stop the back cast a bit higher than normal. —T.E.N.

FIELD & STREAM CRAZY-GOOD GRUB

93 TRY A PLANKED FISH

Here's a method that won't result in half your freshly caught dinner falling into the fire like a roasted marshmallow.

PREP THE PLANK Soak a 3/4- to 1-inch-thick plank of aromatic wood—you can use cedar, oak, or hickory—in water for one to two hours. The plank should be slightly wider than the fish and long enough so that you can prop it up beside the fire in a near-vertical position. Preheat the plank by placing it upright near the fire until it is very hot.

PREP THE FISH Season the fish to taste and secure it to the plank with a couple of nails—drive one into the head and place the second one near the tail.

PROP IT UP Stand the plank up in front of the fire, with the fish tail down. Never flip the fish; monitor the fire to provide a slow cook until flesh flakes in the thickest part of the body. —T.E.N.

94 TOTE YOUR OWN BOAT (LIKE A MAN WITH A TITANIUM SPINE)

It doesn't take Herculean strength to hoist an 80-pound canoe onto your shoulders for a solo carry. The trick is to roll the canoe up your thighs first, then perform a bit of carefully timed clean and jerk to use momentum to lift the boat above your head. It's easy once you know how to do it—and incredibly impressive to perform in front of a crowd. —T.E.N.

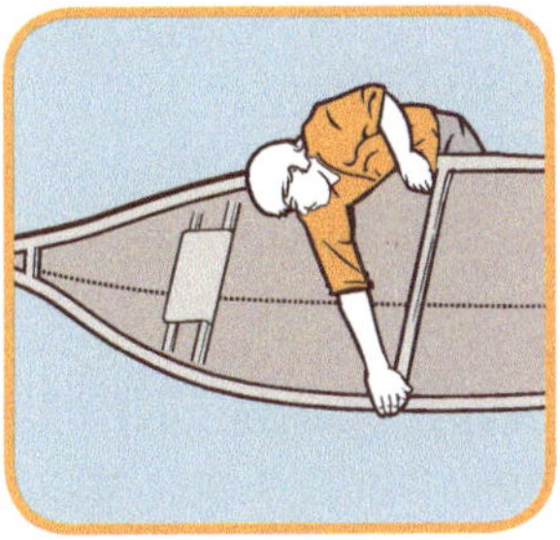

STEP 1 Face the canoe amidships and turn it so that it stands on the gunwale, the bottom resting against your knees. Bend your knees and roll the canoe up on your thighs, with your right hand grasping the far gunwale right at the center thwart and the left hand gripping the near gunwale. Stop and take a breath.

STEP 2 Rock slightly backward two or three times and, on the last rocking motion, push the canoe up and over your head, using both your thighs and your arms.

As your right elbow crosses your face, push with your left arm, straighten your bent legs, and lean back slightly to balance the weight.

STEP 3 When the outside gunwale rises above eye level, lower your head slightly and twist your body to the right. At the same time, push the outside gunwale upward. Now lower the canoe gently with the center thwart resting on the back of your neck. Move your hands slightly forward on the gunwales to fine-tune balance.

95 PADDLE A TANDEM CANOE SOLO

Do it wrong and you look like the single biggest goofball on the lake. But do it right and bystanders will swoon at your power and grace.

GO BACKWARD Turn a tandem canoe around and then paddle it from behind the center thwart.

GET LOW AND LEAN Kneeling slightly off-center keeps your center of gravity low and puts your paddle closer to the water than if you sit upright. A slight lean gives the boat a long, keel-like profile, which makes a huge difference.

CHOP CHOP Get started with short, powerful strokes right at your hip. Once the canoe is underway, lengthen the strokes for a steady cadence. —T.E.N.

96 SHOOT A FLY

If it's hunting season, then it must be time to start thinking about fishing—especially if you like to tie your own flies or bucktail jigs. Many commonly (and not so commonly) hunted birds and animals can and will provide prime fly-tying materials, as long as you know what to clip, pluck, or cut, and how to store and maintain the stuff. To preserve hides, you simply need to salt the patch of fur you wish to keep. If you're saving bird feathers, store them in a zippered plastic bag or screw-top jar. To keep matched feathers from curling or getting smashed, tape the quills together, and you'll have a perfect pair for streamer tails.

The most common natural material for lures is the tail of a whitetail deer. Here's the 4-1-1 on preparation.

STEP 1 Before you convert a whitetail's white tail into jigs or streamers, there's some prep work you'll need to do. Start by skinning the tail. First, split the underside with a fillet knife to within a few inches of the tip. Then peel back the skin, wrap the tailbone with burlap, grasp it firmly, and pull the bone free. Continue the incision to the tip of the tail and scrape away all flesh and fat. Rub with salt or borax and freeze.

STEP 2 To dye the hairs, soak the tail overnight in water and dishwashing detergent, rinse, and dry completely. Mix a solution of sugar-free powdered drink mix (such as Kool-Aid™), water, and vinegar at a ratio of 2 ounces vinegar to 1 cup water. Pour this into a glass jar and submerge the tail. Place the jar in a larger pot of gently boiling water for 20 minutes to an hour or more. Check often for color. Remove the tail, blot, and tack to a piece of plywood to dry. —T.E.N.

ANIMAL	FLY MATERIAL	FLY PATTERN
Elk	Bull body hair	*Elk Hair Caddis and parachute wings*
Whitetail deer	Bucktail, natural or dyed	*Body and wings for Clouser and Deceiver patterns; tails for bucktail jigs*
Rabbit	Fur strips	*Leech, Rabbit Candy patterns; guard hairs for white streamer throats*
Gray squirrel	Tail hairs	*Dry-fly tails and wings, crayfish legs*
Red squirrel	Red, black, and gray tail fur	*Collar on tarpon streamers*
Wild turkey	Secondary wing quills	*Wings for caddis, hopper, and Atlantic salmon patterns*
Wood duck	Barred body feathers	*Classic streamer patterns, tails on dry emergers*
Ringneck pheasant	Rooster tails	*Knotted grasshopper legs*
Sharptail grouse	Body feathers	*Pheasant Tail Nymph tails*
Ruffed grouse	Neck feathers	*Patterned body on tarpon flies*
Hungarian partridge	Neck and body feathers	*Hackles for wet flies*

97 SURF CAST A COUNTRY MILE

Make a good "off-the-beach" cast, and the stripers beyond the breakers will learn to fear your truck. You'll need a shock leader of three times the test of your fishing line—as well as plenty of beach.

STEP 1 Face the water, with your left foot forward. Twist your upper body 90 degrees to the right, and look away from the water. Drift your rod tip back and let the sinker or lure drop to the ground at the 3 o'clock position. Move the rod to about the 1 o'clock position. Drop the rod tip down until your left arm is higher than your right. Reel in the slack.

STEP 2 Start with your right arm straight. With the sinker or lure on the beach, rotate your body at the hips, rod still behind you but moving in a smooth circular pattern, trending upward. Rotational energy fires the cast.

STEP 3 As your body straightens, shift your weight to the left foot, pull your left arm sharply down and in, and push with your right arm. Practice the timing of the release to straighten out a curve in the cast.

—T.E.N.

98 CATCH EVERY FISH THAT BITES

Fish the first cast with as much focus as the sixth or seventh. People walk up to a pool and throw the line in. They're not ready. Make that first cast count, and when you're that close, treat all line tension as fish. Don't hesitate and think, "Oh, that's not a fish. Maybe next time." That was next time. —T.E.N.

99 BUMP BAITS OFF AN UNDERWATER CLIFF

Contour trolling is deadly. Walleyes herd baitfish against sharp dropoffs and walls and then cruise the breaks for targets. Approach these sharp breaks with your boat. As soon as the bottom starts coming up, turn away at a 30- to 45-degree angle. Your baits will still be swinging into the breaks as you turn, and they'll actually dig right into the wall, drag for a few seconds, and then drop out of the sand or rock and dart away. Wham! Many times that erratic action will trigger a bite you'd never get otherwise. —T.E.N.

100 CHOOSE THE RIGHT BLADE

The configuration of spinnerbait blades dictates how the lure moves through the water. And that, of course, dictates in large measure whether a bass will ignore your lure or suck half the pond into its gullet during a boat-swamping strike (which would be a good thing).

There are three basic configuration styles. Round Colorado blades are akin to pimping your spinnerbait ride: They pump out tons of vibration, which makes them a go-to choice for stained water, and they impart the most lift to the lure, so they'll run more shallow than others. Willow-leaf blades create more flash than vibrating fuss, so you'll want to use them for clearer conditions. Willow blades also spin on a tighter axis, so they'll clear weeds more cleanly than others. Indiana blades are a compromise; they look like an elongated Colorado blade. Or a roundish willow-leaf. Nothing simple when it comes to bass fishing. —T.E.N.

Colorado blade

Indiana blade

willow leaf blade

willow leaf blade

101 TOW A CANOE WITH A BOAT

Towing a canoe behind a motorboat is a neat trick, giving anglers a way to haul gear and have a boat ready to portage into remote waters. But a towed canoe can flip almost without warning. Make things go smoothly by towing with a harness that provides the pull from beneath the canoe's keel line.

STEP 1 Turn the canoe so that it will be traveling stern-first. This helps by putting the seat closer to the towing vessel. Use water jugs to provide 40 to 50 pounds of ballast behind the center thwart.

STEP 2 Attach a towline bridle to create a towing point at the canoe's keel. Tie a large butterfly loop in the rope; this is one end of the bridle. Wrap the bridle under the canoe and fasten the loop and one tag end to the seat thwarts. The knot itself should remain under the keel.

STEP 3 Connect the towing end of the rope to the midpoint of a Y-harness attached to the corners of the tow boat's transom. Retain about 30 feet of line between the tow vessel and canoe—enough slack so that you can fine-tune the length if needed.

STEP 4 Watch the canoe carefully, make gradual turns, and do not cross strong wakes. —T.E.N.

102 TAKE A JAW-DROPPING FISH PHOTO

No matter where you land your fish of a lifetime, here's a fool-proof way to capture the moment. Talk your partner through these steps and then smile for the camera:

SET THE SCENE Move away from water muddied by the fight, and keep the fish in the water as much as possible, moving it gently back and forth to keep fresh water washing through its gills. Position the lure in the fish's mouth the way you want it to appear, or remove it. And clear the scene of clutter—drink cans and extra rods and reels, for example. Anything bright or reflective in the scene can act as a focal point for the eyes and inadvertently draw the viewer's attention away from the fish.

MODEL BEHAVIOR Have the angler remove sunglasses and hat, or, at the very least, tip the hat up a bit to prevent a dark shadow from appearing on the face. A shirt with color will add pop to any photo. Muted greens and blues, though, might blend in to foliage or the big sky, and should be avoided if you don't want the subject to fade into the background.

FIRE AWAY Have the angler kneel in the water, supporting the fish with both hands. Meter off of the fish and then have the angler dip the fish into the water. Take a shot as the fish comes up out of the water, streaming droplets of water. Try it again with the flash dialed in to the fill-flash setting. —T.E.N.

103 BACK A TRAILER WITHOUT LOOKING LIKE AN IDIOT

Backing a boat trailer down a ramp isn't all that hard, but like establishing proper lead in wingshooting, it takes practice. The key fact to bear in mind is that the trailer will always go in the direction opposite the tow vehicle. This causes a great deal of confusion and is one of the main reasons you see guys jockeying up and down the ramp with a trailer that seems to have a mind of its own. Here's an easy way to master the maneuver.

STEP 1 Find a big empty parking lot where you can learn to gain control over your trailer without worrying about a long line of irate fishermen behind you. After you shift into reverse, place your left hand on the bottom of the steering wheel (remove fly-tying vise first!). When you move your hand to the right (which turns the steering wheel and front tires to the left), the trailer will move to the right (a). And when you move your hand to the left (which turns the steering wheel and front tires to the right), then the trailer will move to the left (b).

STEP 2 Move slowly. Most beginners back up too fast. If the trailer starts to move in the wrong direction, stop. Pull up, straighten the trailer, and start again. Trying to correct a wayward trailer will only make matters worse. Once you master the parking lot, you're ready for the ramp.

It takes a little getting used to (and your brain will fight you at first), but it works.
—S.L.W.

a

b

104 REPLACE TRAILER BEARINGS ON THE SIDE OF THE ROAD

Burn out boat trailer wheel bearings while on the road and you'll face lost fishing or hunting opportunities, long hours hitching rides to nearby towns, longer nights in fleabag motels, and painful repair bills. That is unless you're prepared with a bearing fix-it kit and the know-how to use it.

ASSEMBLE A FIRST-AID KIT
In a surplus ammo can, place spare bearings, races or "cups," seals, a seal puller, marine-grade bearing grease, a small notepad and pencil, and these instructions. Stow it in your boat.

DISASSEMBLE Remove the grease cover or Bearing Buddy–type cap. Remove cotter pin from spindle nut, remove the nut, and the entire hub should slip off the axle. There are two sets of bearings: one on the inside and one on the outside. Remove them. Tap out the grease seal. If you're unfamiliar with the process, sketch out which parts come off in which order.

CLEAN Clean all the old grease from the bearings, hub, and axle spindle. Wipe away what you can with paper towels and then use mineral spirits or kerosene. Inspect the parts carefully: Look for rust spots, cracks, or bluish staining that indicates overheating. Replace if necessary.

REPACK Hold the bearing with the fingers of one hand, and place a glob of marine bearing grease in the palm of the other hand. Now work the grease into the bearing cage, turning the cage to lubricate each bearing. Put a thin coating of grease onto the spindle and inside of the hub.

REASSEMBLE To replace the grease seal without bending it, position it in the grease bore, place a piece of wood across it, and tap the wood lightly with a hammer. Now reverse the disassembly process, replacing all items in the opposite order.

GO PROFESSIONAL Unless you're 100 percent confident of your ability to get it right, have a mechanic look at your handiwork once you're home. —T.E.N.

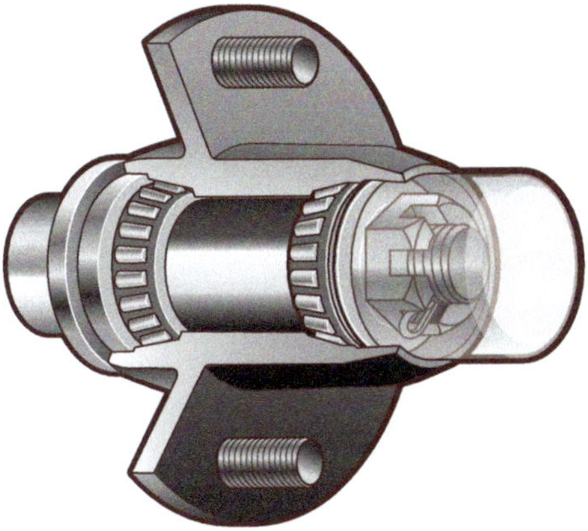

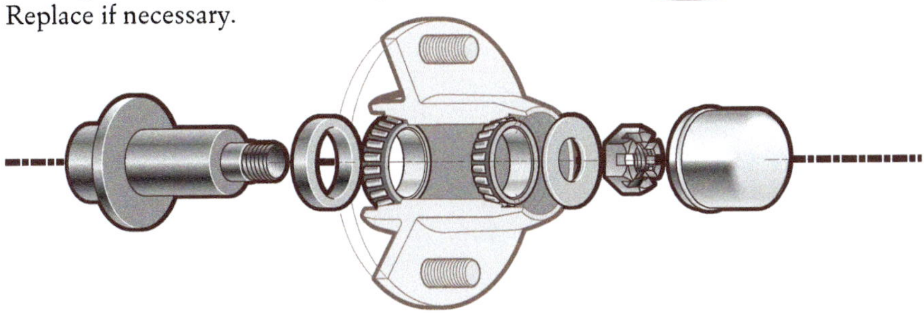

105 FIX A FUSSY MOTOR

Our outboard motors take us to fish- and game-rich waters and woods. And sometimes they leave us there. Modern motors don't give broken-down boaters a whole lot of options, but these five first-aid tips might get you back to the dock when your motor doesn't want to take you there.

TERMINAL BREAKDOWN Loose battery connections lead to corrosion buildup and arcing—which means you're going nowhere. Finger tight isn't tight enough. Scrape the battery terminals clean with a knife blade and tighten the wing nuts with pliers so they bite into the terminal (1).

BACKWOODS NITRO Starter fluid isn't an everyday solution, but sometimes it's the only way to get home when a carburetor-equipped motor seems to have given up the ghost. It's not hard to jerry-rig some with an empty plastic soda or water bottle: Pour gas in, prick a small hole in the top, and screw it back on. Now you can shoot atomized fuel into the carburetor (2).

HOSE WOES Fuel-line hoses are notorious for kinks, dry-rot patches, and collapsed sections. Rebuild them by cutting out the bad part and reusing the hose clamps to reattach the pieces—or use zip ties or fishing line to tie them tightly (3).

SCRUB THE PLUGS To clean fouled spark plugs, remove the plugs and rinse any goop you find from the firing end with gas. Scrape off burned carbon deposits with whatever's handy: a swatch of sandpaper, small knife blade, a hook sharpener, or even a fingernail file (4).

FUEL-PUMP BYPASS If the outboard quits with its primer bulb full of fuel, the problem could be a fuel pump. Bypass it by pumping the primer bulb continuously (5). You'll limp, but better that than a bivvy in the bottom of the boat. —T.E.N.

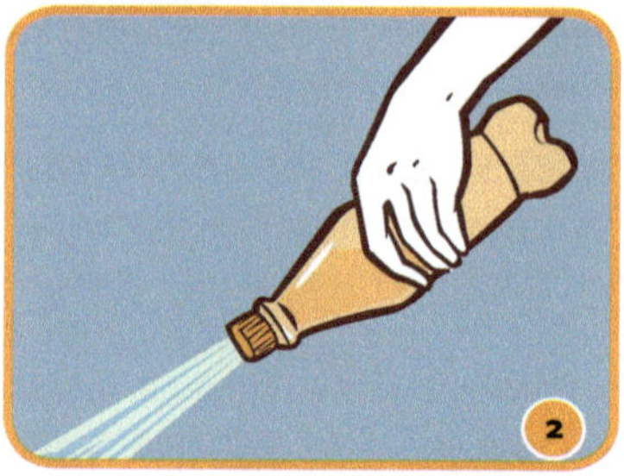

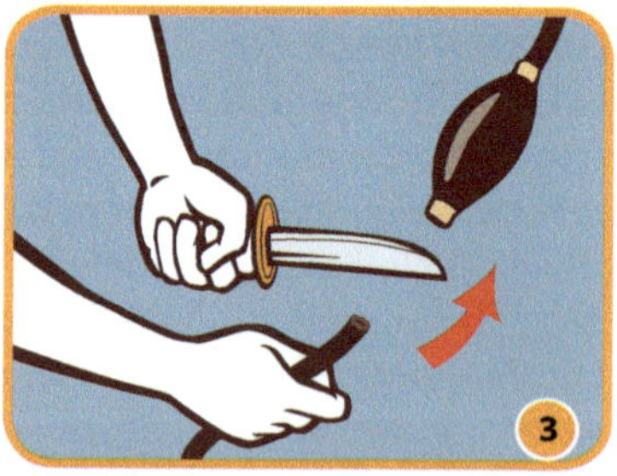

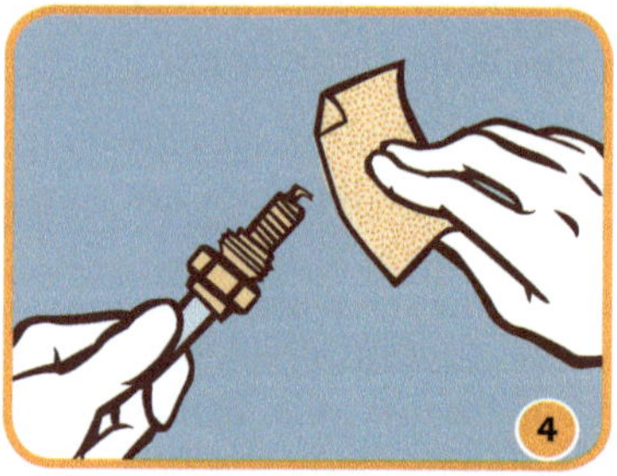

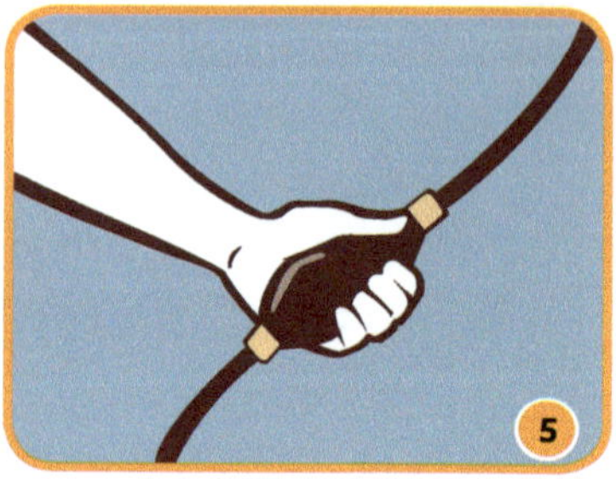

106 FISH EVERY SQUARE INCH OF A FARM POND

Farm ponds can be a fisherman's friend, coughing up big bass, bucketfuls of bream, and enough catfish for a church supper. How to get the most out of the experience? Sure, you could sit on a bucket and drown crickets for a few hours, but it's more fun—and often more effective—to target species with a plan in mind.

BASS A cane pole is perfect for stalking hog largemouths. Forgo the live bait for a stout 3-foot leader of 15-pound mono and a strip of pork rind on a bass hook. (An in-line spinner would work great, too.) Slipping stealthily along the pond, jig every stump, log, and patch of lily pads. Or go tandem in a canoe or johnboat, and trade off paddling and jigging duties each time one of you hooks a fish.

PANFISH Midsummer bream have moved off the spawning beds and into deeper water, so add larger split shot to the cane-pole line and go dredging. Start at the pond dam and dabble bait close to drain structures and any fallen trees, and work over any steep banks and the edges of weedlines. Look for places where shallows fall off into the abyss; submerged creek channels and long points are great targets as well. Use a slip bobber to figure out where the bluegills are hanging.

CATFISH Forget those honking huge flatheads grappled out of subterranean caverns. Younger, smaller cats make the best meals and are a snap to catch with a cane pole. About an hour before the fireworks start, toss chum along a stretch of pond shore—dog food will work, as will chunks of old hot dogs left over from lunch. Come back right after sundown, armed with the cane wand and a cooler of chicken livers or shrimp. Treble hooks will hold the liver better than a single hook. —T.E.N

RESOURCES

(a) Pinnacle Performa XT
www.pinnaclefishing.com

(b) Bass Pro Shops Pro Qualifier
www.basspro.com

(c) Redington Delta
www.redington.com

(a) Heddon Spook
www.heddonlures.com

(b) Luhr Jensen Hot Lips
www.luhrjensen.com

(c) PowerBait HeavyWeight Thump Worm
www.berkley-fishing.com

(d) Rapala Original Floater
www.rapala.com

(e) Booyah Vibra-Flx
www.booyahbaits.com

(f) Mister Twister Curly Tail Grub
www.mistertwister.com

(g) Daredevle Spoon
www.eppinger.net

(h) Kalin's Triple Threat Grub
www.unclejosh.com

(i) Southern Pro Lit'l Hustler
www.southernpro.com

(j) Blue Fox Vibrax Spinner
www.bluefox.com

(k) Smithwick Rattlin' Rogue
www.smithwicklures.com

FIELD & STREAM

In every issue of *Field & Stream* you'll find a lot of stuff: beautiful photography and artwork, adventure stories, wild game recipes, humor, commentary, reviews, and more. That mix is what makes the magazine so great, what's helped it remain relevant since 1895. But at the heart of every issue are the skills. The tips that explain how to land a big trout, the tactics that help you shoot the deer of your life, the lessons that teach you how to survive a cold night outside—those are the stories that readers have come to expect from *Field & Stream.*

You'll find a ton of those skills in this book, but there's not a book big enough to hold them all in one volume. Besides, whether you're new to hunting and fishing or an old pro, there's always more to learn. You can continue to expect *Field & Stream* to teach you those essential skills in every issue. Plus, there's all that other stuff in the magazine, too, which is pretty great. To order a subscription, visit www.fieldandstream.com/subscription.

FIELDANDSTREAM.COM

When *Field & Stream* readers aren't hunting or fishing, they kill hours (and hours) on www.fieldandstream.com. And once you visit the site, you'll understand why. If you enjoy the skills in this book, there's plenty more online—both within our extensive archives of stories from the writers featured here, as well as our network of 50,000-plus experts who can answer all of your questions about the outdoors.

At Fieldandstream.com, you'll get to explore the world's largest online destination for hunters and anglers. Our blogs, written by the leading experts in the outdoors, cover every facet of hunting and fishing and provide constant content that instructs, enlightens, and always entertains. Our collection of adventure videos contains footage that's almost as thrilling to watch as it is to experience for real. And our photo galleries include the best wildlife and outdoor photography you'll find anywhere.

Perhaps best of all is the community you'll find at Fieldandstream.com. It's where you can argue with other readers about the best whitetail cartridge or the perfect venison chili recipe. It's where you can share photos of the fish you catch and the game you shoot. It's where you can enter contests to win guns, gear, and other great prizes. And it's a place where you can spend a lot of time. Which is OK. Just make sure to reserve some hours for the outdoors, too.

THE TOTAL OUTDOORSMAN CHALLENGE

If you enjoyed this book, we encourage you to check out the book it was excerpted from, *The Total Outdoorsman.* This collection of 374 skills covering Camping, Fishing, Hunting, and Survival will make you a true outdoors expert. You'll be ready to take on the world—or at least the wild. Go for it. But you might also consider displaying your newly acquired skills in another arena: the Total Outdoorsman Challenge.

Since 2004, *Field & Stream* has ventured on an annual countrywide search for the nation's best all-around outdoorsman—the person who's equally competent with a rifle, shotgun, bow, rod, and paddle, the person who can do it all. And whoever proves he can do it all walks away with the Total Outdoorsman title, as well as tens of thousands of dollars in cash and prizes.

The Total Outdoorsman Challenge is about more than hunting and fishing, though. The event celebrates our belief that the more outdoor skills you have, the more fun you can have in the woods and on the water. It celebrates the friendships that can only happen between sportsmen. Every year thousands of sportsmen compete in the Total Outdoorsman Challenge, and every year many of those competitors meet new hunting and fishing buddies.

So, if you're ready, you should consider testing your skills in the Total Outdoorsman Challenge. (Visit www.totaloutdoorsmanchallenge.com to learn more about the event.) And if you're not sure you're quite ready, you can always read the book again.

INDEX

A - B - C

D - E - F - G

H - I - J - K

L - M - N - O - P

Q - R - S - T - U

V - W - X - Y - Z

CONTRIBUTORS

T. Edward Nickens (T.E.N.) is Editor-at-Large of *Field & Stream* magazine. Known for do-it-yourself wilderness adventures and profiles about people and places where hunting and fishing are the heart and soul of a community, he has chased ptarmigan and char north of the Arctic Circle, antelope in Wyoming, and striped marlin from a kayak in Baja California. He will not turn down any assignment that involves a paddle or a squirrel. Author of the magazine's "Total Outdoorsman" skills features, he also is host, writer, and co-producer for a number of *Field & Stream*'s television and Web shows, among them *The Total Outdoorsman Challenge* and *Heroes of Conservation*. Nickens has been a National Magazine Award finalist, and has won more than 30 writing awards, including three "Best of the Best" top honors awards from the Outdoor Writers Association of America. He lives in Raleigh, North Carolina, within striking distance of mountain trout, saltwater fly fishing, and a beloved 450-acre hunting lease that has been the cause of many a tardy slip for his two school-age children.

Kirk Deeter (K.D.) is an Editor-at-Large for *Field & Stream* and co-writer of the "Fly Talk" blog at Fieldandstream.com. Deeter is also the publisher and editor of *Angling Trade*, the trade magazine covering the fly-fishing industry in North America. He is known for his "gonzo" story angles, from free-swimming Class IV rapids to fly fishing for mako sharks out of kayaks to fishing in the remote Bolivian jungle with natives in dugout canoes. Deeter has earned various awards, including "Excellence in Craft" top honors for his fishing and conservation stories from the Outdoor Writers Association of America. His most recent book, *The Little Red Book of Fly Fishing*, (co-written with Charlie Meyers), was released by Skyhorse Publishing in 2010. He lives with his wife, Sarah, and son, Paul, in Colorado.

Keith McCafferty (K.M.) writes the "Survival" and "Outdoor Skills" columns for *Field & Stream*, and contributes adventure narratives and how-to stories to the magazine and Fieldandstream.com. McCafferty has been nominated for many National Magazine Awards over the years, most recently for his February 2007 cover story, "Survivor." McCafferty's assignments for *Field & Stream* have taken him as far as the jungles of India and as close to home as his backyard. McCafferty lives in Bozeman, Montana, with his wife, Gail. McCafferty loves to fly fish for steelhead in British Columbia and climb the Rockies in pursuit of bull elk.

John Merwin (J.M.) has been the primary author of *Field & Stream*'s fishing features and columns for the past 15 years. In 2008, he extended his angling expertise online to Fieldandstream.com as the co-author of the fishing blog "The Honest Angler." Among other accolades, Merwin was nominated for a National Magazine Award for his story "*Field & Stream*'s Best of Summer Fishing," in the June 2008 issue. He is the former editor and publisher of both *Fly Rod & Reel* and *Fly-Tackle Dealer* magazines. He served for several years as the executive director of the American Museum of Fly Fishing and has authored and edited a total of 15 books on angling, including the best-selling *Trailside Guide to Fly Fishing*. Merwin lives in Vermont with his wife, Martha.

Additional contributors: Joe Cermele, Tom Tiberio, and Slaton L. White.

CREDITS

Cover images Front: Alexander Ivanor (stickbait) Shutterstock (background texture) Back: Left, Jameson Simpson Center, Bryon Thompson Right, Mike Sudal

Photography courtesy of Shutterstock, with the following exceptions: Rick Adair: 65, 90 Barry and Cathy Beck: 18, 74, 87 Bill Buckley: Fishing introduction (fishermen catching fish), 80 Eric Engbretson: 5, 43 Cliff Gardiner and John Keller: 8, 58 (tube jig), 100 Brian Grossenbacher: 13, 27 Alexander Ivanov: 35, 86 (soft plastic, stickbait, spinnerbait, crank bait, surface lure) Bill Lindner: 61 Pippa Morris: 3, 15 (gold ribbed hare's ear, black ant, popping bug, cricket, mini-tube spinner) Ted Morrison: 86 (panfish), 93 T. Edward Nickens: 17, 29, 30 Travis Rathbone: 25 Dan Saelinger: Fishing introduction (tackle box), 7, 38, 49, 82, 84, 86 (walleye, pike, smallmouth, trout, striper)

Illustrations courtesy of Hayden Foell: 103 Alan Kikuchi: Fishing icon Kopp Illustration: 104 Raymond Larette: 23, 65, 68, 94 Daniel Marsiglio: 1, 10, 14, 33, 42, 48, 62, 71, 72, 91, 97, 106 Chris Philpot: 75

ACKNOWLEDGMENTS

From the Author, T. Edward Nickens

I would like to thank all of the talented people who made this book possible, including the *Field & Stream* staff editors who guided this project with great care and insight. *Field & Stream* field editors Phil Bourjaily, Keith McCafferty, John Merwin, and David E. Petzal, and editor-at-large Kirk Deeter, provided unmatched expertise. Just good enough is never good enough for them. I wish I could name all the guides, outfitters, and hunting, fishing, and camping companions I've enjoyed over the years. Every trip has been a graduate course in outdoor skills, and much of the knowledge within the covers of this book I've learned at the feet of others. And last, thanks to my longtime field partner, Scott Wood, who has pulled me out of many a bad spot, and whose skillful, detailed approach to hunting and fishing is an inspiration.

From *Field & Stream*'s Editor, Anthony Licata

I would like to thank Weldon Owen publisher Roger Shaw, executive editor Mariah Bear, and art director Iain Morris, who have put together a book filled with skills that have stood the test of time—in a package that should do the same. I'd also like to thank Eric Zinczenko, *Field & Stream* VP and Group Publisher, for championing the Total Outdoorsman concept in all its forms. This great collection of skills would not have been possible without the hard work of the entire *Field & Stream* team, and I'd particularly like to thank Art Director Sean Johnston, Photo Editor Amy Berkley, former Art Director Neil Jamieson, Executive Editor Mike Toth, Managing Editor Jean McKenna, Deputy Editor Jay Cassell, Senior Editor Colin Kearn, and Associate Editor Joe Cermele. I'd also like to thank Sid Evans for his role in creating the Total Outdoorsmen concept. Finally, I'd like to thank my father, Joseph Licata, who first brought me into the fields and streams and showed me what being a total outdoorsman really meant.

"Of all the outdoor pursuits, fishing may be the most knowledge-intensive. Every day is different. Every hour can change everything. Every species–every single fish–requires a specific set of actions and decisions designed to put forth what seems to be the simplest of requests: Eat this please."

—T. Edward Nickens

Please visit our webite, **www.garethstevens.com**. For a free color catalog of all our high-quality books, call toll free 1-800-542-2595 or fax 1-877-542-2596.

Library of Congress Cataloging-in-Publication Data

Nickens, T Edward.
Field & stream's guide to fishing / by T. Edward Nickens.
p. cm. — (Field & stream's guide to the outdoors)
Includes index.
ISBN 978-1-4824-2300-6 (library binding)
1. Fishing — Juvenile literature. I. Nickens, T Edward.
II. Title.
SH445.N53 2015
799.1—d23

Published in 2015 by
Gareth Stevens Publishing
111 East 14th Street, Suite 349
New York, NY 10003

President, CEO: Terry Newell
VP, Publisher: Roger Shaw
Executive Editor: Mariah Bear
Creative Director: Kelly Booth
Art Director: William van Roden
Designer: Meghan Hildebrand
Cover Design: William Mack
Illustration Coordinator: Conor Buckley
Production Director: Chris Hemesath
Production Manager: Michelle Duggan

Printed in the United States of America
CPSIA compliance information: Batch CW15GS: For further information contact Gareth Stevens, New York, New York at 1-800-542-2595.